Disney
The Never Girls

volume 2: books 4-6

randomhousekids.com/disney
ISBN 978-0-7364-3581-9
Printed in the United States of America

10 9 8 7 6 5 4 3 2

volume 2: books 4-6

Written by
Kiki Thorpe

Illustrated by
Jana Christy

A STEPPING STONE BOOK™
RANDOM HOUSE 🏠 NEW YORK

Never Land

Far away from the world we know, on the distant seas of dreams, lies an island called Never Land. It is a place full of magic, where mermaids sing, fairies play, and children never grow up. Adventures happen every day, and anything is possible.

There are two ways to reach Never Land. One is to find the island yourself. The other is for it to find you. Finding Never Land on your own takes a lot of luck and a pinch of fairy dust. Even then, you will only find the island if it wants to be found.

Every once in a while, Never Land drifts close to our world . . . so close a fairy's laugh slips through. And every once in an even longer while, Never Land opens its doors to a special few. Believing in magic and fairies from the bottom of your heart can make the extraordinary happen. If you suddenly hear tiny bells or feel a sea breeze where there is no sea, pay careful attention. Never Land may be close by. You could find yourself there in the blink of an eye.

One day, four special girls came to Never Land in just this way. This is their story.

Never Land

Pirate Cove

Torth Mountain

Skull Rock

Pixie Hollow

Mermaid Lagoon

"I'm not afraid of a little fog," kate said.
"Why should I be, when I have Cloud?"

The Never Girls

from the
mist

Written by
Kiki Thorpe

Illustrated by
Jana Christy

A STEPPING STONE BOOK™
RANDOM HOUSE 🏠 NEW YORK

Chapter 1

Kate McCrady opened one eye, then the other. Early-morning sunlight streamed across her face.

Kate blinked, still half asleep. Was she in her own bedroom at home? Was she sleeping under the weeping willow tree in Never Land? For a moment, she didn't know. She pushed her tangle of red hair out of the way and saw a large dollhouse in the corner.

Oh, that's right, Kate thought. She was at her best friend Mia Vasquez's house, sleeping over. Lainey Winters was there, too, bundled in a sleeping bag a few feet away.

Kate tried to send them a silent message: *Wake up! Wake up, so we can go back!*

Only a few days before, Kate, Mia, Lainey, and Mia's little sister, Gabby, had found a secret portal to Pixie Hollow, the realm of the fairies on the island of Never Land. Or rather, the portal had found them—even though the path to Never Land wasn't always in the same place, it always seemed to be where the girls could find it.

Kate loved their visits to Never Land. There she had no homework, no chores—nothing to do but explore. Adventure waited around every tree, hill, and bend along Havendish Stream. Kate couldn't wait to go back.

But her silent message didn't work. Lainey let out a gentle snore. Mia turned over, burrowing deeper under her covers.

Maybe a nudge would wake them. Kate stretched so her foot grazed the bottom of Lainey's sleeping bag. She scooted closer, then stretched again. This time, she bumped Lainey's leg.

Lainey sat up, blinking sleepily.

"I was just stretching," said Kate, trying to look innocent. "I didn't wake you, did I?"

"No . . . yes." Lainey fumbled around by her pillow. When she found her glasses, she put them on, a little crookedly. "Is Mia awake?"

"I am now!" cried Mia, pulling the pillow over her head. Kate could only see a bit of her long, dark curly hair poking out. "What time is it? It feels too early to be awake."

"It *is* early." Kate jumped up, leaped over Lainey, and bounced on Mia's bed. "Early enough to get back to Never Land."

Mia glanced at the clock. It said 6:30. "My parents won't be awake until at least seven."

"Exactly," said Kate. "And that could mean hours and hours in Never Land." The girls had discovered that time worked differently on their trips to Pixie Hollow. Hours could pass there, while at home hardly a minute would go by. "Let's go now!"

Mia bolted upright as a thought came to her. "I hope Gabby kept our promise. I hope she didn't try to go to Never Land while we were sleeping."

On their last visit, the portal had closed, and Gabby had been stuck alone in Never Land. After that, the girls had made a promise to always go to Never Land *together*. But Mia was worried that Gabby wouldn't be able to resist going on her own anyway, since the portal was now in her room.

The three girls dressed quickly. Kate pulled her thick red hair away from her face with a barrette without bothering to comb it. Then she, Mia, and Lainey tiptoed across the hall to Gabby's room.

Inside the door, Kate stopped short. "Do you guys see what I see?" she whispered.

Lainey and Mia nodded. A dense mist hung over half the room.

Meanwhile, Gabby slept peacefully on her back, unaware of anything unusual. Her arms were spread wide, as if she were waiting for a hug.

"She looks so sweet," Mia said softly. "Maybe we shouldn't wake her."

Suddenly, Gabby sat up. "What's going on?" she said, looking around. "Why is my room so foggy?"

"I don't know. Something strange is happening," said Mia. "Look at the closet door."

A heavy mist hovered around the doorframe. More fog seemed to seep from

beneath the door—the door that led to
Never Land.

Kate rushed over. "I'll check it out."

"Wait, Kate. We all go together, or we
don't go at all," Mia reminded her.

Kate stopped with her hand on the
doorknob. "Hurry and get dressed, Gabby."

Gabby hopped out of bed. She slipped
a pink tutu and a pair of costume fairy

wings over her pajamas. "Ready!" she announced.

Kate pulled open the door. Gabby, Mia, and Lainey crowded behind her.

Inside the closet, fog swirled from floor to ceiling. It covered Gabby's toys and clothes. Holding hands, the girls stepped through the mist.

Kate heard a tinkling sound, like bells ringing. She took another step. Faint voices floated toward them.

"I hear the fairies!" Lainey said.

The voices grew louder as the girls crept forward. The walls around them curved, becoming the inside of a hollowed-out tree trunk.

Finally, they stepped out from the tree. They were standing on a grassy bank in

Pixie Hollow. At least, Kate *thought* it was Pixie Hollow. It was hard to tell. Fog covered everything.

"I can barely see!" exclaimed Lainey. She wiped her glasses.

Kate shuffled forward a bit, squinting. "There has never been fog in Pixie Hollow before. It's always sunny when we visit."

She didn't see Havendish Stream until she almost walked into it. Now she could see the fairies whose voices they'd heard. They were water fairies paddling birchbark canoes. The fairies called out to one another so their boats wouldn't bump.

"Watch out!"

"Where did this fog come from?"

"Go to the right, Silvermist!"

Spring, a messenger, flew over the

water, shouting to the fairies. "Everyone to the courtyard! Queen Clarion has called a special meeting!

"Oh!" She stopped inches in front of Kate. "I didn't know you girls were here. Better come, too!"

At the courtyard, Kate stared up at the Home Tree. The giant maple, filled with fairy bedrooms and workshops, usually sparkled with fairy glow. But today its branches were hidden in mist.

Around the girls, fairies crowded into the pebbled courtyard. They landed on the low tree branches, where they sat lined up like birds on a telephone wire. They chattered nervously, filling the air with a low hum.

"What's going on?" Kate asked a baking fairy, Dulcie, who was hovering nearby.

"Queen Clarion is worried about this fog. We all are. It is awfully strange weather for Never Land."

"What's causing it?" Kate asked.

Dulcie shrugged. "All I know is it's making the fairies hungry. At breakfast today, everyone ate like it was the Harvest Feast."

"Breakfast?" Kate's stomach rumbled. They hadn't had a chance to eat.

Dulcie winked knowingly. "I'll get you girls some treats right away!" Nothing made Dulcie happier than filling empty stomachs.

Moments later, serving-talent fairies delivered basket after basket filled with blueberry puffs. Each puff was the size of a marble. Kate ate two dozen.

Rain, a weather-talent fairy, flew by

carrying a medicine dropper. She pressed the dropper's bulb to draw in some mist. Then she peered at the droplets inside.

"Sure, it's a mist easter with foggish low bursts," she announced. Then she frowned. "But squalls are down."

"Is that good or bad?" Kate asked. But she was talking to herself. Rain had already flown away.

chapter 2

Mist in the morning, fairies take warning.

Silvermist stood in the courtyard, waiting with the other fairies for Queen Clarion to speak. But her thoughts strayed.

Mist in the morning, fairies take warning. Why couldn't she get that old fairy saying out of her head?

Silvermist tucked her long hair behind her ears. All morning, she'd felt uneasy. She'd been boating on Havendish Stream when the fog came. Silvermist had never seen such a heavy mist before. It had taken all her water knowledge to get her boat to shore without running into anything.

As a water-talent fairy, Silvermist liked water in any form—from dewdrop to rushing waterfall. Usually, just being near it soothed her. But this clammy mist made Silvermist shiver from wing to wing.

Why is it bothering me? she wondered. After all, mist was water, too.

As she thought about it, Silvermist noticed the four Clumsies kneel down behind her. *Girls. Not Clumsies,* she reminded herself. *They don't like to be called that.* She nodded hello to Kate, Mia, Lainey, and Gabby.

"Hi, Silvermist," the tall one, Kate,

said. "What do you think about this fog? You're a water fairy, so you must know what's going on."

Silvermist shook her head. "I'm afraid I don't."

"Well, that's helpful," said Vidia, a fast-flying fairy, as she swept past. "A water talent who doesn't have a clue about the water right in front of her nose."

Silvermist didn't bother to reply. Vidia always had something nasty to say. Still, the remark bothered her. Why *didn't* she know more?

Mist in the morning, fairies take warning.

"Fairies, sparrow men, and guests!" Queen Clarion finally spoke, interrupting

Silvermist's thoughts. "Gather close, so we can see each other more clearly."

Everyone edged forward.

"We don't know how long the fog will last," the queen said. "But it's too dangerous to fly in weather like this. There could be accidents. So for now, all fairies are grounded."

A murmur rippled through the crowd.

"What?" Vidia's voice rose above the others. "You can't mean fast-flying fairies, too? Why should we be punished?"

"No one is being punished, Vidia," the queen replied. "It's for your own safety."

"Couldn't there be exceptions?" Vidia asked, her voice sugary.

Out of the corner of her eye, Silvermist noticed Kate eagerly move closer, to see if she was "grounded," too.

Queen Clarion thought for a moment. "You're right, Vidia. There should be a few exceptions."

Vidia gazed around at the other fairies, a superior smile on her face.

"We'll need some fairies to stay on lookout, to make sure everyone is safe," Queen Clarion continued. "The scouts—and only the scouts—may fly."

Hearing this, the fairies grumbled, especially Vidia, who scurried away using her wings to help her walk faster.

After the meeting, fairies milled around in the courtyard. They seemed nervous about going anywhere on foot.

Fawn, an animal-talent fairy, came toward Silvermist. "Have you seen Beck, or any of the other animal talents?" she asked. "We need to bring in the dairy mice, but it could take ages walking. We'll have to work together to herd them."

"Can I help?" asked a voice behind Silvermist.

"Oh, Lainey, that would be wonderful," Fawn said. "You can cover much more ground than we can. And you can practice your mouse calls."

Lainey beamed, happy to be of use. She turned to Kate. "Do you want to come?"

Kate shrugged. "I don't speak Mouse. I'll find something else to do."

"Come with us!" Hem, a sewing-talent fairy, called from down by Kate's feet.

"Yes!" echoed Mia, taking Gabby's hand. "We're going to make some new doll clothes. Hem is going to help us."

Kate shook her head. "I'm not really

in the mood for sewing . . . ," she began, when a loud rumble rolled through the sky.

All the fairies stopped what they were doing and looked up. But there was nothing to see but fog.

"What was that?" Silvermist asked.

The rumble grew louder.

Myka, one of the scout-talent fairies, took off into the soupy air. Right away, Silvermist lost sight of her.

"The fog is moving," said Myka. Her voice came down faintly through the mist. Thunder sounded again, drowning out the rest of her words. But they didn't need to hear her. The fairies could see for themselves that the fog was roiling, gathering into great big swirls.

A gust of wind kicked up. Trees
swayed. The fairies clung to each other.
"Is it a storm?" Dulcie cried. Storms were
rare in Never Land.

Suddenly, a shrill whinny split the air.

"That sounded like it came from the
meadow!" cried Fawn.

Everyone ran toward the meadow. The fairies on the ground scrambled over tree roots and darted around clumps of flowers. Several fairies caught rides with the girls, who could run much faster with their long legs. Silvermist joined a group of fairies riding on Kate's shoulder.

The scouts flew and arrived at the meadow first. The girls got there just afterward. They all stood at the edge of the woods. No one wanted to go closer.

A huge cloud was rolling across the grass. It churned like rushing flood waters. The thunder was deafening. The earth trembled.

Then, as quickly as it had come up, the noise died down. The cloud blew away. In its place stood a herd of silver-white beasts with wispy manes and tails that trailed into mist. One of them shook its head. Another flicked its tail. Droplets of rain flew off them.

"Horses!" Kate murmured, her eyes wide.

"Not just horses," whispered Silvermist. "Mist horses."

Chapter 3

Kate stood at the edge of the meadow, gazing at the horses. Her friends, the fairies, and everything else fell away as she stared.

The horses were huge, and yet they looked light as air. The ends of their long manes and tails seemed to disappear into the mist. Their eyes were a ghostly gray. To Kate, they looked as if they'd come straight out of the sky, as if the wind and rain had brought them to life. Even in a magical place like Never Land, the horses seemed otherworldly.

"Mist in the morning, fairies take warning," whispered a voice at Kate's ear. It was the water fairy Silvermist.

"There's some sort of legend about the mist horses," Silvermist went on, almost as if she was talking to herself. "I think they bring trouble."

Several fairies nearby turned to look at her. "Trouble," repeated a sparrow man, sounding worried. Others frowned.

What kind of trouble could these creatures bring? Kate wondered. They looked so beautiful and peaceful.

"You know, I'm probably confusing mist horses with sea horses," Silvermist said quickly. "I'm sure it's nothing."

The animal-talent fairy Fawn spoke up. "I'll talk to the horses. Find out where they're from and why they're here."

Fawn fluttered closer to one of the animals. She stopped so she could look it in the eye and swung her long ponytail like a mane. Then she let out a *hmph*, followed by a snort and a whinny.

Kate thought she sounded just like a horse.

But the mist creature ignored her. Fawn tried again. This time, the horse turned its back. Fawn tried another horse, but it also turned away.

Fawn sighed loudly. "They're not telling me any—"

Suddenly, one horse flicked its tail, striking Fawn.

"Oh!" Fawn spun through the air like a top out of control.

Silvermist and Tinker Bell raced to her. They each caught hold of one of Fawn's hands. They whirled along with her until, bit by bit, they slowed. At last, they were able to land on a rock.

"Fawn, are you okay?" Tinker Bell asked.

Fawn nodded, dazed. "I—I think so."

"It's time to leave the meadow," Queen Clarion said. "It's too dangerous here."

Kate's heart sank. Leave? Now, when the horses had only just arrived? But most of the fairies seemed perfectly happy to go.

On the way back, Dulcie was already talking about the light-as-mist meringues she wanted to bake. Other fairies planned a game of hide-and-seek. "It will be extra fun in the fog!" said a sparrow man. Fawn, still too dizzy to walk, was riding on Lainey's shoulder.

Kate fell into step beside Mia. "I don't see why we have to go," she complained.

"It's probably better. They do seem kind of dangerous," Mia said with a glance at Gabby.

Dangerous? Kate thought. "Exciting" was a better word. Of course, if you were a five-year-old—or a five-inch fairy—it was a different story. Then it made sense to stay clear of the horses. But everyone always said Kate was tall for her age. She wouldn't be in any danger.

"So now you can help us with the doll clothes," Mia went on cheerfully. "We can start by sorting the petals and silk threads."

Mia kept talking, but Kate stopped paying attention. She really didn't want to go back to the Home Tree and sew doll clothes. Or even play fairy hide-and-seek.

The fairies, able to squeeze into knot-holes or inside flower petals, always won.

Kate wanted to run and jump! She always chose soccer over quiet games during recess at school. After sitting at a desk for hours, she needed to move. That was how she felt now, too.

Those horses! Kate could tell they also loved to run and jump. They were so . . . so *alive*!

Kate stopped. "I'm going back for another look," she told Mia.

"What?" Mia said, startled.

"I'll just be a minute," Kate promised. "I'll meet you at the Home Tree."

Before Mia could say anything else, Kate turned and ran back to the meadow.

She stood at the edge of the trees, afraid to go any closer.

The horses were still there, almost hidden in the mist. One bright, silvery mare stood at the edge of the herd. As Kate watched, the mare suddenly kicked up her hooves. She moved away from the other horses, galloping around the meadow's edge.

As the horse neared Kate, she slowed to a trot.

She sees me! Kate realized.

The mare stopped a few feet away. For an instant, Kate held her gaze. *What would it feel like to touch a mist horse?* she wondered.

Kate inched closer. Then closer still. Slowly, hardly daring to breathe, she reached out her hand. She half expected it to go through the horse, as if she were made of air.

But the mare was solid. Kate stroked her neck lightly, feeling the velvet fur and the muscle underneath.

She feels like a real horse! Kate thought. Or at least what she imagined a real horse would feel like. Before now, Kate had never touched a horse. The closest she'd come was riding the carousel in City Park, near her home. But she very much wanted to ride this horse.

Kate glanced around to make sure no one was watching. If she tried to ride and then fell off, she'd be so embarrassed! Then, feeling brave and silly at the same time, she took hold of the horse's mane as gently as she could. The horse flicked her ears but didn't move.

But the mare was much taller than Kate had realized. She had no idea how to climb on!

Looking around, Kate spotted a thick tree branch a few feet above her. Maybe if she could climb the tree, she could lower herself onto the horse's back.

"Don't move," Kate whispered. She scrambled up the tree trunk, glad for the time she'd spent climbing trees in Never Land, on lookout with the scouts. Kate inched along the branch until she was more or less above the horse. The mare, nibbling at the meadow grass, didn't seem to notice.

Using all the strength in her arms,

Kate lowered herself from the tree branch. Now she was dangling in the air above the horse.

"Steady now," she murmured. But just then, the horse took a step forward.

"No!" Kate gasped. Afraid it was about to run away, she let go quickly, landing squarely on the mare's back.

The horse took off. On the verge of falling, Kate reached out and grabbed a handful of the horse's long mane. She bounced all over its back. Her teeth rattled together. She expected to hit the ground at any moment. But she didn't.

At last, Kate pulled herself more or less upright. She tightened her grip on the horse and squeezed with her knees to try to balance. The horse sped up. Kate let out a panicked squeal, but she stayed on.

"Hey!" she cried. "I'm riding!"

The faster the horse ran, the smoother her gait became. She left the meadow and headed over a hill that led to more forest.

It seemed to Kate as if they were swimming through the air. She felt a thrill travel from the tips of her toes to the top of her head. Were the horse's hooves even touching the earth? Kate couldn't tell.

"How do I steer?" she wondered aloud. Kate leaned slightly to one side, as she would to turn her bike. She tugged gently on the horse's mane. The horse began to turn.

"Yes!" Kate pumped a fist in victory. Then she grabbed quickly for the horse's mane again. She needed to hold on with two hands to keep from falling off.

At last, the horse slowed to a trot and then to a walk. They were nearing the meadow again. "Thank you for the ride. You can go back to your herd now," Kate said.

But as they came through the trees, Kate saw that the meadow was empty. The horses were gone! In the distance, she heard whinnies and the sounds of branches snapping.

At that moment, the scout Myka swooped down from a treetop. "What are you doing here?" she asked Kate. "And on a horse!"

Kate grinned. "I was just going for a ride," she said casually. "Did you see the herd from up there?" She pointed to the tree where Myka usually stood lookout.

Myka shook her head. "It's hard to see anything in this fog," she admitted. "I did catch a glimpse of something moving. It could have been the horses. If it *was* them, they're heading toward Vine Grove, north of here."

"Vine Grove," Kate repeated. Perhaps she could go there, too.

Myka frowned as if she knew what Kate was thinking. "It's outside Pixie Hollow."

"I'll bring this horse to her herd. Then I'll come back to the Home Tree." Kate figured that she could get to Vine Grove in no time on the horse. Then she could run back on foot before anyone missed her. "I'll be fast," she told Myka.

"I don't think that's a good idea," Myka said. "Wait here and—"

But Kate was already galloping away.

Chapter 4

Silvermist hovered in front of a high shelf in the Home Tree library. She was trying to find a book about the mist horse legend.

She looked over the leaf-books on the Myths and Legends shelf. "Maybe it should be called *Mists* and Legends." Silvermist laughed at her own joke, then glanced around, afraid she might be bothering another fairy. But she was alone.

"So where might this old story be?" Silvermist said. She pulled a book from the shelf. It was titled *Hailstones in the Hollow and Other Odd Weather Fables.*

She flipped through the pages. When she saw the words "mist horse," she stopped and skimmed the page.

"Oh no!" Silvermist dropped the book with a thud. No wonder that warning

had been echoing in her head all morning. According to the legend, the fairies were in danger!

It's just a legend, Silvermist reminded herself. Picking up the book with shaking hands, she placed it back on the shelf. *It's a story, that's all.* But Silvermist had learned that superstitious old fables sometimes had a kernel of truth. If even a little bit of the legend was true, she had to warn the queen.

After leaving the library, Silvermist hurried to the Home Tree and rushed up to the queen's chambers. She knocked, but there was no answer. She knocked again. Nothing.

Growing impatient, Silvermist flung open the door.

"Oh cockleshells," she groaned. No one was there.

But through the open sea-glass window, she heard fairies talking. "I saw Kate at the meadow." Silvermist recognized Myka's voice. "She was riding a horse."

Silvermist darted back the way she'd come and went outside. Myka stood on a low branch, talking to Queen Clarion. Mia, Lainey, and Gabby were there, too.

"That can't be right," Mia was saying. "Kate's never ridden a horse in her life."

"Queen Clarion—" Silvermist began. But the queen held up a hand.

"Just a moment, Silvermist," she said. "Myka was telling us something important. Are you sure it was Kate, Myka?"

"Of course I am!" Myka said. "I spoke to her. And she *was* riding one of the mist horses. She was leaving Pixie Hollow."

"No!" Silvermist gasped. This time, everyone turned to look at her.

"I went to the library," she explained. "I found an old legend about the mist horses. . . ."

Silvermist paused and glanced at the girls. After all, the legend might not be true, and she didn't want to frighten them.

"Go on," the queen said.

"Well, I read that the horses enchant their riders, so they keep riding and riding," Silvermist said.

"You mean, they can't get off?" Mia asked.

Silvermist nodded. "The rider believes the horse is loyal and obedient. But it's a trick. It's the rider who obeys the horse, as if under a spell."

"What does that mean?" Gabby squeaked in alarm.

Mia exchanged a horrified look with Lainey. "It means Kate might be in trouble."

"We have to find her!" Lainey said.

"But what about the fog?" asked Myka. "Even the scouts can't see in it."

"We'll need someone who can find their way through it," Queen Clarion said. "Silvermist, you have my permission to fly to find Kate."

"Me? Oh!" Silvermist hadn't expected to lead the mission. She opened her mouth to explain that she didn't understand the fog any better than anyone else, then closed it. After all, Kate needed their help.

"We should leave now," she said to the girls. "The longer we wait, the harder it could be to find her. Who knows how far Kate can get on a horse. Myka, are you coming?"

Myka shook her head. "Some of the animal-talent fairies are missing. We think they got lost trying to find the dairy mice. The scouts are out looking for them."

Silvermist squared her shoulders. So she would have to lead them on her own.

"When I last saw Kate, she was headed toward Vine Grove," Myka said.

Silvermist turned to leave, but the queen stopped her, adding, "And for Never's sake, everyone, be careful."

Chapter 5

"Come on, girl!" Kate urged the horse. Shapes loomed up from the mist, becoming trees and rocks that passed in a blur. Riding in the fog reminded Kate of riding a bicycle at night. She couldn't see things until they were almost on top of them. Still, the horse seemed to know where she was going. They managed not to hit anything.

As they rounded a small pond, the horse slowed. Kate reached down and patted the horse's neck. She felt like she'd been riding her whole life. And what a way to explore Never Land!

Kate looked around, trying to get her bearings. Were they close to Vine Grove? The island, cloaked in fog, seemed as mysterious as the mist horse. Kate had the feeling that anything could happen. That she could see anything. Go anywhere.

Why shouldn't *I go anywhere?* Kate thought. *I can explore a bit first and then bring the mare back to her herd. One little detour won't make a difference.*

Besides, Kate reasoned, there was really no need to go right back. The horse—*her* horse—seemed to be enjoying the ride as much as she was. The longer Kate rode, the more certain of it she felt.

The horse was a wild, free creature.

She made Kate feel wild and free, too.

"Let's go to the beach!" Kate cried. She turned the horse around sharply. The mare's hooves kicked up puffs of mist, like little clouds.

"Cloud," Kate said. "That's what I'll call you." The name seemed as light and free as the horse itself.

They cantered over a hill and through a grassy field. A sand dune appeared in the fog. Cloud sped up one side of the dune. Kate leaned low over the horse's neck as they raced down the other side, onto the beach.

The mist was heavier here. It rolled up to the beach with every wave.

They rode along the sand. When they came to the water's edge, Cloud whinnied

loudly and charged into the surf. Waves splashed Kate's legs. She laughed out loud.

But Cloud didn't stop. Just when Kate thought she'd go under with the next wave, Cloud whirled around, taking Kate back up the beach.

Still laughing, Kate slid off Cloud's back. She removed her shoes, emptying water from them. Her jeans were soaked, but she was too excited to feel cold.

"Is anyone there?" a fairy voice called. It sounded like Myka.

Kate groaned inwardly. Now she'd have to explain what she was doing here, when she was supposed to be looking for the herd in Vine Grove.

As she opened her mouth to call back, another voice rang out. It sounded very close by, just on the other side of Cloud.

"Okay, you found me," a voice drawled with fake sweetness. "Congratulations, Myka. You caught me flying. But why go through all the trouble of tracking me down? I'm not bothering anyone here. Can't a fast-flying fairy have a little fun?"

Vidia! Kate realized. Myka hadn't been talking to Kate. She was talking to Vidia. Cloud, who blended into the mist, must be shielding Kate from their view.

"No one's trying to get in your way, Vidia," Myka said. "I was scouting for lost fairies."

"Well, I'm not lost. I know exactly where I am."

Kate stood still. She hoped Vidia and

Myka wouldn't notice her. This time, Myka would insist she go back. Then Cloud raised her head and snorted.

"Are you coming down with the fairy flu, Vidia?" Myka asked. "It wouldn't be a surprise in this damp weather. You should go home and have a nice hot cup of dandelion tea."

"I didn't sneeze," Vidia snapped. "*You* did. Don't try to trick me."

"Trick you?" Myka repeated, confused. "I'm not trying to do anything but keep you safe."

"Tell you what," Vidia said, her voice

sugary again. "If you can catch me, I'll go back with you."

Kate heard the fast fluttering of wings, then Myka sighing.

Silence fell. Had Myka flown off, too? Kate waited a few moments longer, then decided she and Cloud were alone.

I'll leave now, too, Kate thought. She could take a shortcut, going around the pond the other way to get to Vine Grove. Then she'd go back to the Home Tree.

"Okay," Kate whispered into Cloud's ear. "Let's get you to the herd."

There was no tree nearby. But this time, as Kate took hold of Cloud's mane, she managed to pull herself up with only a bit of struggle. Kicking her legs, she belly-flopped onto Cloud's back, then wriggled around so she was upright.

"Is anyone else here?" Myka called. "Water fairies? Sparrow men?" She paused. "Kate?"

But Kate didn't hear her. She was on her way to Vine Grove.

*

On horseback, Kate neared a thick copse of trees. Long green vines twisted around trunks and looped from branches.

"That must be Vine Grove!" Kate said.

Kate rode into the trees, following the sounds. As they went deeper into the grove, the trees grew closer together. Creeping plants covered the ground. The path became hard to follow.

Kate ducked her head as vines brushed

her face. Between the fog and the leaves, she could barely see.

Ahead, vines tangled together like a thick green wall. Cloud strained through.

"Oh!" Kate struggled, pushing . . . pulling . . . batting at leaves and stems. But the vines caught her up like a net, holding her fast.

Cloud kept moving, and Kate, trapped in the vines, swung into the air.

"Cloud!" she called. The horse stopped a few feet away. She looked back at Kate and whinnied, as if to say, *What on earth are you doing?*

Suspended in midair, Kate struggled and flailed. But she couldn't free herself from the vines. She needed Cloud to pull her out.

She called again. "Cloud! Here, girl!"
This time, Cloud stepped closer.

Slowly, Kate worked one arm free. She
stretched but couldn't reach Cloud. "Just
a little bit closer," she coaxed. The horse
toed the ground but didn't move.

All Kate could do was throw her legs
forward and back and begin to swing.

With every swing, she got a little closer to the horse. At last she'd worked herself forward far enough that the fingertips of her free hand grazed Cloud's mane. One more swing, and Kate flung her arm around Cloud's neck.

"Go!" she shouted.

Cloud took off, pulling Kate along with her.

The vines around Kate snapped free of the trees. The force swung her out of the vine trap and over Cloud's head, as if she were jumping from a swing when it had reached its peak. She landed hard on the ground.

Kate stood up shakily. Her bangs fell into her eyes, and as she reached up to swipe them away, she realized she'd lost her barrette. She spent a few moments searching for it, but it was nowhere to be seen in the dense undergrowth.

Kate turned in a circle, trying to get her bearings. Ahead, the trees thinned out a little. She could see the shapes of large animals moving among them. The herd!

"Go on, girl," she said to Cloud. "Your friends are right over there!"

But Cloud didn't move.

Why doesn't she go to them? Kate thought. Something was wrong.

Kate made her way toward the herd. As she drew closer, she could see the animals more clearly. They weren't horses after all. They were deer.

She'd been following the wrong herd!

Where were the mist horses?

Kate looked to where the trees thinned out even more. *If I were a horse, I'd rather be out in the open than in a dense forest,* she thought.

"Let's keep going," Kate told Cloud. They'd find the herd. It wouldn't be fair to Cloud to give up.

And besides, Kate was having too much fun.

chapter 6

Back in Pixie Hollow, Silvermist and the girls set out toward Vine Grove. Silvermist flew in front. The girls walked single file behind her, following a narrow path. The path was faint and overgrown, more a deer trail than anything. But it was the quickest way to Vine Grove that Silvermist knew.

Vine Grove was to the north of Pixie Hollow. The trail went through the woods and around a small pond. When Silvermist came to the edge of the pond, she stopped.

There in the mud were two crescent-shaped marks. *Hoofprints!* Silvermist realized.

"What is it?" asked Mia, coming up behind her.

"There," Silvermist said, pointing. "They're from a horse's hooves, I'm sure of it."

"If the herd came this way, there'd be more tracks. So it must be from the horse Kate is riding!" Lainey said. "Let's follow them."

"The thing is, they're headed south, toward the ocean," Silvermist said. "*Away from Vine Grove.*"

Mia frowned. "Myka said Kate was headed *toward* Vine Grove. We should go there."

"But this is a clue!" Lainey countered. "Don't you think we should follow it?"

Both girls looked at Silvermist. She realized they were waiting for her to decide what to do.

Silvermist looked down at the tracks, thinking. The hoofprints did seem like a good sign. On the other hand, Kate had told Myka that she was going to Vine Grove. Which way was right?

Silvermist took a deep breath and closed her eyes. *Trust your instincts,* she advised herself. *If I were on a mist horse, where would I go?* Behind her lids, Silvermist saw waves crashing. She felt the tug of the ocean.

Silvermist opened her eyes. "We should go to the beach," she said.

With Silvermist once again in the lead, the group set off. Before long, the woods gave way to marsh. They climbed over a dune, slipping and sliding down the soft sand on the other side. Fog still hid everything around them. But they could hear waves breaking and seagulls squawking, and Silvermist knew they'd reached the beach.

"Stay close," she instructed. "We don't want to get separated in the fog."

"Kate?" Mia shouted. "Are you here?"

"Kate! Kate!" Lainey and Gabby joined in. They walked up and down the water's edge, calling and searching. But there was no sign of Kate.

"She's not here," Gabby said finally.

"Maybe we should have gone to Vine Grove after all," Lainey said, glancing at Silvermist.

Silvermist nodded, feeling a knot in her stomach. She'd been so sure that this way was right. But maybe it was only her feeling for water that had drawn her toward the ocean. Maybe her instincts had let her down.

And now they had lost so much time!

"We'd better hurry," she said, "or we may never catch up with Kate."

The girls and Silvermist retraced their steps away from the beach. This time, Silvermist didn't stop to check for prints. She didn't want to waste another second.

Soon enough, they came to a thick wooded area. Long vines hung from the trees, twisting around trunks and plants.

"This must be Vine Grove!" Mia said, racing toward the trees. "Kate! Where are you?" she cried.

But once again, no one answered her.

The girls walked among the vines, looking all around. Silvermist flew close to the ground. She scoured the undergrowth for some sign that Kate had been there. But she saw nothing.

"I don't understand," Mia said. "If Kate's not here, where is she?"

Silvermist swallowed hard. "There's something I haven't told you. About the legend—"

She was interrupted by a shout. "Over here!" Lainey cried. "I found something."

They followed Lainey's voice through a tangle of vines. Lainey stood on the other side. She pointed to the ground. "These vines were trampled."

"Something big must have done this," Mia said, examining the vines. "Maybe a horse. What do you think, Silvermist?"

Silvermist nodded. "It's possible."

A short distance away, they found another tangle of broken vines. Between the leaves, something gleamed.

"Look!" Gabby cried, bending over to pick it up. "A barrette."

"It's *Kate's* barrette," Mia said. "So she *was* here!"

Silvermist blushed, her glow turning orange with embarrassment. She was sure she'd flown right past this spot before. How could she have missed something as obvious as a Clumsy's barrette? She was starting to wonder if she should be leading the girls at all.

"Silvermist," Gabby said, "what should we do now?"

Silvermist hesitated. She couldn't trust her instincts. They had led her astray once already. She needed a real clue.

A movement among the trees made Silvermist's heart skip a beat. She turned toward it, hoping to see Kate. But it was only a deer. The deer gazed silently at them for a moment. Then it turned and bounded away, shaking droplets from the wet leaves around it.

"I wish I could speak Deer," Lainey said. "I could have asked if it had seen Kate."

"Hmm," said Silvermist, not really listening. The deer had given her an idea.

She began to fly slowly over the ground, looking closely at the leaves and blades of grass.

"What are you doing?" Mia asked.

"The leaves and grass are covered with droplets of water from the mist," Silvermist explained. "So if something as big as a horse passed through here, it would shake the water off . . . like this!" Silvermist pointed to a path through the damp grass.

The girls squinted. "I don't really see anything," Lainey said.

But Silvermist could see it clearly. Each blade of grass was wet on one side and dry on the other. "A large creature has come this way."

"Are you sure it was Kate and the horse?" Mia asked. "And not a deer or something?"

"I'm not sure it was Kate," Silvermist

admitted. "But it was bigger than a deer. And right now, I'm afraid that it's our only clue. We have to keep going."

Before it's too late, she added to herself.

chapter 7

Cloud galloped down a hill covered with sweet-smelling primroses. Kate could just see the yellow blossoms peeking out from the drifting mist.

Kate giggled with delight and flung one arm into the air, as if she were riding a roller coaster. This time she wasn't afraid of falling off. "Yeehaw!" she yelled.

The ground leveled, and they trotted past a noisy waterfall. The rushing water gurgled and hissed, dropping from a rocky ledge into a deep blue pool.

A butterfly fluttered in front of them. Its bright blue color was startling in the sea of white mist. Kate sneezed, and the butterfly spiraled away in the whoosh of air.

Never Land was even more amazing than Kate had imagined—animals, flowers, fog, and all. She spurred Cloud on, eager to see more.

But wait, she reminded herself. *We have to search for Cloud's herd.*

And then what?

Kate had never cared much about having a pet, unlike Mia, who loved her cat, Bingo, and Lainey, who loved all animals. But now that she and Cloud

were together, Kate wanted a horse. She wanted *this* horse. If she and Cloud could stay together, Kate would have days like this all the time.

Oh, if only there was some way I could keep her! Kate thought.

"Caught you, Clumsy," a voice purred in her ear.

Kate jumped. She twisted around and saw Vidia flying next to her.

"Look who's taking in the sights of Never Land," Vidia said. "Seems we're both far from home. Lost, are you?"

"Of course not," Kate snapped. Truthfully, she wasn't sure how far away from Pixie Hollow she was. But she felt certain that when it was time to return, she could find her way. "I'm bringing this horse to its herd."

"I don't care much what you do," Vidia said. "But I'm heading back to Pixie Hollow. The fog seems to be getting worse in this direction."

Kate frowned. She didn't want any advice—especially not from Vidia.

"I'm not afraid of a little fog," she said. "Why should I be, when I have Cloud?"

"You really think you've trained a wild horse?" Vidia snickered.

Kate grinned. "Watch this! Go, Cloud!"

At that, Cloud took off, leaving Vidia far behind.

This time, they rode until Kate's arms and legs ached. Her belly grumbled with hunger. She hadn't had anything to eat except Dulcie's blueberry puffs, hours earlier. She thought Cloud must be worn out, too. But strangely, the horse never seemed to get tired.

When Kate spied an apple tree rising out of the mist, she stopped and hopped off the horse. She twisted two apples from the tree and held one out for Cloud.

The horse sniffed the apple but didn't take it.

"I thought horses were supposed to like apples," Kate said. "Oh well, more for me." She bit into an apple, crunching loudly. "My legs are tired." Kate looked around for somewhere to sit.

A short distance away, she spied a big black rock. "Let's rest over there," she said.

Kate peered at the rock. Had it just moved?

The rock stretched, growing larger.

Kate froze, stifling a cry. That was no rock. It was a bear!

The bear rose to its feet. Kate hoped it hadn't noticed them in the mist. If they could hide somewhere, maybe they'd be safe. Kate glanced around. The only thing she saw was the apple tree.

The bear started to lumber toward them. Kate dropped the apples she was holding and inched herself behind the tree. She stood as still as a statue, afraid to run and draw the bear's attention. Maybe, by some miracle, it would pass them by.

The bear advanced until it was so close she could hear it grunting. She could see the droplets of mist on its thick black fur.

Reaching the apple tree, the bear rose on its hind legs. It lifted its giant paw to strike—

At a beehive! Kate almost laughed out loud in relief. The bear was only reaching for the beehive hanging from a branch!

The hive fell to the ground, spilling honey. Angry bees swarmed around the tree. They buzzed through the mist, darkening the orchard. One of them stung Kate on her arm. She covered the sting

with her hand and gritted her teeth. They had to get out of there!

The bear was digging its paw into the hive. Kate saw her chance. She rushed to Cloud and scrambled up onto her back. "Go!" she murmured. "Go!"

Without a backward glance, they raced away.

When she thought they had gone far enough, Kate caught her breath. "Whoa!" she told Cloud. "Slow down now."

She grinned as Cloud slowed to a walk. How well Cloud understood her!

"I wish you could be my horse, always," Kate said.

Ahead, Kate saw a wide, rushing river—the biggest one she'd ever seen in Never Land.

It must be Wough River, she thought. *The big river that runs from Torth Mountain to the sea.* Kate hadn't been there before, but she'd heard the fairies talk about it. She knew she was far, far from Pixie Hollow. It would take her ages to walk back.

That is, if I can even find my way, Kate thought. She realized she'd been wrong when she'd spoken to Vidia—she had no idea which direction Pixie Hollow was in. All the landmarks she'd passed were hidden in the fog.

For the first time since she'd left Pixie Hollow with Cloud, Kate started to feel worried. She knew she needed to find her way home as quickly as possible.

And yet she hesitated. The truth was, she wasn't ready to say good-bye to Cloud.

Cloud suddenly lifted her head. She looked alert.

"What is it?" Kate asked.

A whinny rang out from across the river. Then another. It was the herd! Kate nudged the horse with her heels.

When they reached the edge of the water, Cloud didn't even pause. The fast-moving water frothed around her hooves as she charged across. Kate couldn't tell if the river was shallow or if Cloud was actually striding across the surface.

Within moments, Cloud was scrambling up the far bank. The herd was just ahead. Kate's thoughts of returning to Pixie Hollow melted away.

Chapter 8

As the day wore on, Silvermist tried her best to follow the trails through the damp grass. But doubts constantly tugged at her mind. Sometimes the trail disappeared. Other times it seemed to go in two directions at once. And, as Mia had pointed out, were they even really following Kate? With every turn, Silvermist doubted her choices.

If only there were some way to be sure!

Once, when Silvermist peered through the fog, she thought she saw a dark-haired fairy flying fast.

"Vidia!" she called, hoping the fairy might have seen Kate. "Is that you?"

But if Vidia heard her, she didn't reply.

At last, in a valley, Silvermist lost the trail completely. She stopped and looked around. A short distance away stood a crooked old apple tree. A broken beehive lay on the ground beneath it. A few bees buzzed around the tree.

Silvermist was tired. Her wings ached. She could see that the girls were exhausted, too.

"It's useless!" Mia complained, flopping down to the ground. "Kate's on a horse. We'll never catch up with her." Her forehead furrowed. "It's just like Kate to go running off and leave us behind to worry about her."

"We can't give up," Silvermist said.

"Mia's right," Lainey agreed. "We should go back to Pixie Hollow and wait for Kate there. After all, Never Land is an island. If she goes around it, she'll end up back there eventually. Right?"

"There's a part of the legend I didn't tell you," Silvermist said. "I didn't want you to be afraid. But Kate is in danger. According to the legend, once the mist horse has a rider, it never lets her go. It will spirit her away to the clouds—forever."

The girls stared at her, wide-eyed. "That means we might never see Kate again?" Lainey whispered.

Mia leaped to her feet. "We have to go now!"

At that moment, they saw a large, dark shape coming toward them through the mist. *Not a horse,* Silvermist thought, peering at it. *Something bigger . . .*

"Bear!" Gabby gasped.

"Run!" cried Mia.

"No! Don't!" Lainey whispered. "That will make it want to chase you."

The girls froze. The bear was coming closer. It was no more than twenty feet away from them now.

"I'm scared," said Gabby.

"Somebody *do* something!" hissed Mia.

Silvermist fluttered in distress. She was only a tiny fairy! How could she stop a huge bear? Maybe she could throw an apple at it? Or should she fly right at the bear and try to distract it? She flittered back and forth, unsure what to do.

Just then, she heard a string of high-pitched squeaks. Silvermist looked around. She realized the squeaks were coming from Lainey.

The bear heard them, too. It rose onto its hind legs and sniffed the air. It seemed confused.

A moment passed. Lainey squeaked again. The bear turned and lumbered away.

The girls stayed frozen until the bear was out of sight. Then everyone whooshed

out a sigh of relief. "I didn't know you could speak Bear!" Mia said to Lainey.

"I can't," Lainey admitted. "I was speaking Mouse. I don't know why—it just came out."

"What did you say?" Gabby asked.

Lainey grinned sheepishly. "I said, 'I've lost my brothers and sisters. There are twenty more like me. Have you seen them?'"

"He probably thought you were the biggest mouse he'd ever seen," Silvermist said with a chuckle.

Everyone laughed. But their laughter quickly faded. "Is Kate going to be okay?" Gabby asked.

Lainey glanced at Silvermist with a worried look. "I hope so."

Mia was collecting apples from the tree. Suddenly, she stopped and sucked in her breath. "Look!" she said, holding an apple core up by its stem. "It's been eaten. And not by a bear."

"It could have been Kate!" Lainey said. "That means she did pass through here!"

Silvermist looked to the far end of the valley. "I think Wough River is just ahead. She'll have to stop to rest at some point. Let's hope we can catch her there."

When they reached the river, Silvermist lighted on Gabby's shoulder. They stood on the rocky bank, looking at the water rushing past. Silvermist took a deep breath and let the sound soothe her nerves. Water always made her feel calmer.

"She's not here," Mia said, looking as if she might cry. "And how will we ever get across?" The shore on the other side of the river was nearly lost in the fog.

"Hello?" came a voice from the mist.

Silvermist looked around. No one was there.

"Silvermist?"

"Did you call me?" Silvermist asked the girls.

They all shook their heads. *Am I hearing things?* wondered Silvermist.

"It's me." The fog swirled in front of Silvermist. She made out the shape of one wing, then another. Then Myka appeared. She was wearing a cottony top and pants and a cotton-ball hat. "I'm in camouflage so predators won't see me. You can't be too careful in this fog," she explained.

"Have you seen Kate?" Mia asked quickly.

Myka shook her head. "I haven't seen anyone except Vidia. And even she was on her way back to Pixie Hollow. The fog seems to be worse over here."

So it was *Vidia I saw,* thought Silvermist.

"The mist is retreating around Pixie Hollow," Myka said. "The Home Tree is all clear. Maybe that means the fog is leaving Never Land."

The girls looked stricken. "Oh no. Kate!" said Mia.

"What is it?" Myka asked.

Silvermist explained the myth to Myka. "But maybe there's still time," she said. Being near the water was helping her think more clearly. "The fog follows the mist horses. And it's as thick as we've seen it here. Perhaps that's a sign that the horses are nearby. And maybe Kate is with them."

"Do you really think so?" Lainey asked.

Silvermist took a deep breath. Even

though she'd made mistakes, she'd gotten the girls this far.

"I'm almost sure of it," she told the others.

Lainey squinted at the water. "Okay," she said slowly. "But how do we get to the other side?"

Chapter 9

The river was wide and the current strong. Silvermist knew the girls couldn't swim across. And they couldn't fly like fairies.

She looked around. Her eyes fell on the remains of an old tree that had fallen upstream. It looked almost long enough to stretch from one bank to the other.

"Maybe we could use that log as a bridge," she said.

The girls walked up to the log and strained to lift it. It didn't budge.

"Good thing I have a little extra fairy dust," said Myka. "This will lighten our load." She sprinkled the dust on the log.

"One, two, three, lift!" shouted Silvermist.

The girls raised the log easily. It stood straight up like a telephone pole.

"Now let it drop!" Silvermist cried.

They did, and the log fell across the river with a huge splash. Silvermist grinned. She'd been right about the length. The far end landed on the opposite shore.

Lainey eyed the log nervously. "It looks slippery."

"That's one thing I can help with,"

Silvermist said. Using her water magic, she drew water from the wood, drying off the top of the log. A stream of droplets trailed behind her like a banner until the tree's surface was dry.

"I'll go in front," Mia said. "Gabby, stay right behind me."

Mia stepped out onto the log. Gabby followed, flapping her arms. "If I start to fall, I can use my wings."

Mia grimaced as the log trembled. "Be careful, Gabby. Remember, some of us don't *have* wings."

"We can think of it like a balance beam," Lainey said. "Like in gymnastics class."

Silvermist had no idea what Lainey was talking about. She knew the girls went to school on the mainland. Maybe they learned how to walk on logs there.

The girls put one foot in front of the other, stepping carefully. Slowly, they made their way across.

"Look at me, Silvermist!" Gabby giggled. "I'm a balance-talent fairy!"

Mia hopped off the log, landing on the muddy bank. Laughing, Gabby leaped into her waiting arms. But as she did, her feet pushed the log away from the shore.

"Ahhh!" screamed Lainey, who hadn't quite reached the end. Her arms flailed. She began to lose her balance.

"Jump!" cried Silvermist.

Lainey leaped as the log broke free. Her feet splashed down in the water, but her hands landed in the mud on the bank. Mia and Gabby scrambled to pull her onshore.

"Are you okay?" Mia asked.

"I think so," Lainey said shakily as she climbed to her feet. She looked down at her soaked jeans and dirty shirt. "Just wet—and muddy. Yuck!" She grinned up at Mia. "I don't know how we're going to explain *this* to your parents when they wake up."

Mia grinned back, and Silvermist sighed with relief. That had been a close one.

"Do we go left, right, or straight?" Lainey asked, turning to Silvermist.

Silvermist looked around. The fog was thicker than ever to her right. She was sure now that her guess about the horses had been correct.

"Follow me!" she said.

*

Kate's heart thudded. Cloud had climbed up and up a steep, narrow trail. They were close to the herd. That meant they were close to the end of their journey, too.

She could hear the horses, but she couldn't see them. High whinnies and low nickers echoed through the mist. The fog was so thick here, it was like walking through cotton. The ground beneath them felt thin and rocky—Kate could hear stones clattering beneath Cloud's hooves. A chilly wind was blowing.

Then, suddenly, Kate saw the herd. The horses all lifted their heads to watch Kate and Cloud's approach. In the swirling mist, the animals looked ghostly.

Cloud rode Kate into the center of the herd. The horses circled them, some of them nuzzling Cloud in greeting. An electric feeling coursed through Kate. Was this really happening to her? Even the animal-talent fairy Fawn hadn't been able to talk to the horses. And yet, Kate was being welcomed into their midst.

Kate wished this moment would never end.

But then she heard voices. Not horses, or even fairies, but human voices. At first, she couldn't make out what they were saying. Then, quite clearly, she heard her name: *"K-a-a-ate!"*

It was Mia!

Then she heard Lainey and Gabby, and small, thin fairy voices, too. They were all calling out to her.

She couldn't see her friends through the fog, so she steered Cloud toward the sound of their voices. Suddenly, Cloud stopped so fast that Kate fell forward against her mane. Cloud's front hoof dislodged a stone. Kate listened as it bounced down . . .

and down . . .

and down.

At that moment, the wind shifted, briefly clearing the mist. Kate gasped. She and Cloud stood at the edge of a narrow ledge. Before them lay a deep, rocky canyon. On the other side of the canyon were Kate's friends, separated from her by the huge chasm.

Mia, Lainey, and Gabby were waving and screaming. Now she could hear their cries more clearly.

"Get away from there, Kate! The horse is . . ."

Kate couldn't hear the rest. She tried

to get Cloud to back up, but the herd was crowded in behind them. There was nowhere to go.

Cloud took a step forward. They were going to fall!

"No!" shouted Mia.

"Stop!" cried Lainey.

"Kate!" screamed Gabby.

But it was too late. Cloud stepped off the edge.

Chapter 10

Kate squeezed her eyes shut. She braced herself, expecting to drop like a stone. Instead, she felt a gentle wind against her face.

Kate opened her eyes. Cloud was galloping in the air high above the canyon. They were flying!

Cloud rode the wind. Legs pumping, she climbed up above the fog right into the clear blue sky.

Kate couldn't say a word. She was breathless with excitement. They were really and truly flying!

The other mist horses galloped around them. With a sound like rolling thunder, the herd stampeded across the sky.

At last, Kate found her voice. She cried out, a loud, joyful whoop. She felt like the queen of the sky!

Just when it seemed as if they might leave the earth for good, Cloud began to turn. The herd followed. They raced back and landed lightly on the narrow strip of land, across the chasm from where they'd come. Cloud had brought Kate to her friends.

Kate slid off the mist horse and grinned. "Did you guys see that?"

"Kate!" Mia rushed over and wrapped her in a hug. Lainey and Gabby joined her. "You're all right!"

"Of course I'm all right," said Kate, surprised. "Why wouldn't I be? And what are you all doing here anyway?"

"We thought the horse had kidnapped you!" Gabby said.

"You mean Cloud?" Kate patted the horse's neck. "Of course not. She's my new best friend."

Silvermist and the other girls explained everything—the mist horse legend, the scary thought that Kate might be spirited away, and the long journey they'd taken to find her.

"I was afraid we'd never find you, after my many wrong turns," Silvermist said.

"I even went to the beach, thinking you might be there."

"I *did* go to the beach," Kate said. "Before I went to Vine Grove."

"Silvermist, you were right all along," Lainey said.

Myka smiled at her water-talent friend. "It seems you're a better tracker than you realize."

Silvermist's glow turned pink as she blushed at the compliment. "So I guess the legend was wrong," she said. "The mist horses aren't dangerous. I wonder how that idea ever came to be."

"I'll bet I know. Maybe once upon a

time someone *did* ride away with the mist horses forever. After riding with Cloud, I can understand why they would want to." Kate laughed as Cloud nuzzled her cheek. "But I can't believe you were worried. My horse would never do anything bad."

Mia looked puzzled. "Did you just say *my* horse?"

Kate gave a sheepish smile. "I guess I did. And in a way, she is mine—like I'm hers. But just now, when we were riding, flying up in the air, I realized Cloud doesn't need a rider. She needs to be free. She needs to run wild with her herd."

Kate hugged the mist horse around the neck, holding on tightly for a long moment. Then she stepped back. "Go on now," she said. "Go be with your friends. I'll never forget you."

Cloud looked Kate in the eye and whinnied. Then she took off, climbing into the sky once again. The other horses galloped toward her. They met in a flurry of hooves and mist. Together, they raced away.

"Look!" Silvermist exclaimed. "The fog is lifting!"

The mist rose like a curtain. They could see the landscape clearly now: the cliffs, the canyons, and the ocean in the distance.

Kate, her friends, and the fairies watched the horses until all they could see were the last thin wisps of their tails trailing across the sky.

"Those clouds will be bringing rain," Silvermist added. "We should get back to the Home Tree." She winked at Gabby. "Before our wings get wet and we can't fly."

Gabby laughed. "You know I can't fly without fairy dust! Anyway, I'd rather walk with Kate." She reached for Kate's hand.

Kate squeezed Gabby's hand in her own. She was glad to be back with her friends. And in a way, she was glad to have two feet on solid ground again.

"What about you, Kate?" Silvermist asked. "Are you ready?"

Kate nodded. "I've had enough adventure for one day." She smiled at Silvermist. "Lead the way."

The filmy fabric looked a bit
like her own fairy wings.
It looked...magical.

wedding wings

Written by
Kiki Thorpe

Illustrated by
Jana Christy

A STEPPING STONE BOOK™
RANDOM HOUSE 🏠 NEW YORK

chapter 1

Gabby Vasquez hurried up the stairs to her room. She had news—the kind of fizzy, exciting news that wouldn't stay bottled up inside. She just had to tell someone about it!

In her bedroom, Gabby raced to the closet. She threw the door open wide, shouting, "Guess what, everyone?"

She stepped inside, pulling the door shut behind her. The closet was very dark, but it was a friendly sort of darkness. She could smell the sweet scent of orange blossoms and hear water trickling over rocks.

Gabby shuffled forward. Soon she saw a window of light. A moment later, she emerged into the sunshine of Pixie Hollow.

Hop-two-three. Gabby skipped from rock to rock, crossing Havendish Stream. She wriggled between two wild rosebushes on the far bank. Her costume fairy wings caught on a thorn. Gabby quickly checked to make sure the fabric hadn't ripped. Then she plunged ahead, stumbling a little in her hurry.

As she came over a small rise, she could see the Home Tree, the great maple where the Never fairies worked and lived. The fairies' golden glows shone among the leaves, making it seem as if the branches were filled with stars.

"Tink! Prilla! Everybody! Guess what?" Gabby shouted as she raced toward the tree.

On a high branch, the art-talent fairy Bess looked up from her painting. Prilla, the clapping-talent fairy, awoke from her doze in a cozy magnolia blossom. The pots-and-pans fairy Tinker Bell stuck her head out of her teakettle workshop. The garden fairy Rosetta set down her miniature gourd watering can. And Dulcie, a baking-talent fairy, dusted the flour from her hands. They all flew to the courtyard.

"What's going on?" Prilla asked as Gabby ran up to them, breathless.

Gabby bounced on her toes with excitement. "There's going to be a wedding," she announced. "And I'm the star!"

"A wedding?" cried Dulcie, wringing

her apron. "Why didn't anyone tell me? I haven't baked a thing!"

"Not here, silly," Gabby said. "At home. Our babysitter Julia is getting married, and I'm going to be the flower girl!"

"Is that anything like being a flower-talent fairy?" Rosetta asked.

"Kind of," said Gabby. "I'm in charge of all the flower magic. And I get to wear this special dress." She did a twirl so the fairies could admire her brand-new, pretty pink flower girl dress.

"It's lovely!" exclaimed Rosetta, who adored dresses of all kinds.

"I have this basket, too." Gabby held up a little basket with a bow tied around the handle. "And I throw flower petals. Like this." Gabby pretended to pull a handful of petals from the basket and throw them.

"Hmm." Rosetta frowned.

Gabby stopped. "What's the matter?"

"Why not practice with some *real* flowers?" Rosetta suggested. She plucked a bundle of daisies that were growing nearby and shook the petals into Gabby's basket.

Gabby threw a few of the petals. They plopped to the ground.

"Well, that's not very interesting," said Tink.

"Wouldn't it be nicer if the petals moved around a little?" suggested Bess. She dove into the basket and came up with an armful of petals. When she threw them into the air, they swirled like snowflakes.

Gabby gasped. "How did you do that?"

"It's easy. You just need a bit of fairy magic." Bess shook her wings over the basket. A sprinkle of fairy dust rained down on the petals. "Try it again."

This time the petals almost leaped from Gabby's hand. They fluttered in the air before drifting to the ground.

The fairies nodded happily.

"Oh yes!"

"Much nicer!"

"Just lovely."

Gabby smiled and threw another handful just to watch the petals swirl. "Can I have some fairy dust to take with me to the wedding tomorrow? Please?"

"I don't see why not," Tink said. She darted away. In a moment she was back with a little thimble bucket. It had a tight-fitting silver lid. "I made the lid myself," Tink said proudly. "You won't lose a speck of dust."

Gabby peeked inside and saw the shimmery fairy dust. "Thank you," she said, tucking the thimble into the pocket of her dress.

"I've heard of weddings, but I've never seen one," said Prilla. She traveled to the world of Clumsies—or humans—more than most fairies. "What are they like?"

"A wedding is when two people get married," Gabby told her. "They say 'I love you.' Then they give each other rings and everybody claps. And then . . ." Here, Gabby's knowledge of weddings became somewhat murky, but she continued, "Then they float away on a cloud and live happily ever after!"

"Very dramatic," Bess said approvingly.

"Will there be food at the wedding?" Dulcie asked.

"Yes! Really fancy food, like onion rings. And a cake this big!" Gabby stretched her hands up over her head. To the fairies, the cake seemed enormous.

"My!" Dulcie exclaimed.

"Will there be music and dancing?" Tinker Bell asked. "At fairy parties there's always dancing."

Gabby had no idea if there was dancing at a wedding. But her imagination had taken over now. "Everybody dances! And there are butterflies everywhere! And a chocolate waterfall!" Gabby spun on her toes, inspired by her own vision of how wonderful the wedding would be.

Prilla's freckled face took on a dreamy

look. "It sounds marvelous. I wish I could see it."

"You could come with me!" Gabby suggested.

"Gabby! Gabby?" a voice called out from the direction of Havendish Stream.

Everyone turned as Gabby's older sister, Mia, came into view. As soon as she spotted Gabby, her face darkened.

"Uh-oh," murmured Gabby.

"I knew it!" Mia said, charging over. "Gabby, you're not supposed to come here by yourself. Remember what happened last time?"

Gabby remembered. She'd gone to Never Land alone and gotten stuck there when the hole between their two worlds had briefly closed. After that, Gabby,

Mia, and their friends Kate McCrady and Lainey Winters had made a rule that they would always go to Never Land together—a rule that Gabby, in her excitement, had forgotten.

"It was just for a minute," she said. "I was going to come right back."

"She was telling us about the wedding," said Prilla, trying to be helpful.

Mia rolled her eyes. "Gabby hasn't stopped talking about it all week. It is exciting, though," she added. "It's our first wedding ever."

"But I'm the only flower girl," Gabby pointed out.

"That's just because you're the littlest. Flower girls are supposed to be little. I don't know why," Mia said. A tiny wrinkle formed between her eyebrows, but it was gone a moment later. "I wish we could stay," she told the fairies. "But it's bath time for Gabby, and Mami's looking for her. We'll be back soon, though. I promise."

Taking Gabby's hand, Mia began to walk toward the passage that led back to their world. "I can't believe you," she whispered to Gabby. "We only have one rule about Never Land and you've already broken it. And you made me break it, too. What will we tell Kate and Lainey?"

"We don't have to tell them," Gabby said quickly. She was sorry she'd forgotten their agreement. She didn't want Kate and Lainey to be upset. "You won't tell them, will you?"

"We'll see," said Mia.

They had almost reached Havendish Stream when Gabby stopped so suddenly she yanked her sister backward. "I almost forgot," she said. "I have to tell the fairies how to get to the wedding."

She started to turn around, but Mia stopped her. "The fairies can't come to the wedding," she said.

"But I want them to see me be a flower girl!" Gabby cried.

"There will be lots of people there tomorrow," Mia said. "What if someone sees them? No one can know about Pixie Hollow. It's our secret."

Mia let go of Gabby's hand as they crossed the stepping-stones in Havendish Stream. But at the foot of the hollow fig tree, Mia stopped. She knelt down so she was looking Gabby in the eye. "You can't say a word about fairies or magic to anyone tomorrow. Promise?"

Gabby gazed back into her sister's brown eyes. "Okay," she said. "I promise."

*

After the girls left, the fairies went back to what they'd been doing. Rosetta flew off to water the lilies. Tinker Bell returned to her workshop. Dulcie, inspired by Gabby's description, headed to the kitchen to try her hand at a seven-layer thimble cake.

Bess flew back to her matchstick easel. She had been working on a painting of a dew-covered spiderweb. The dewdrops were so plump and glistening they seemed about to roll right off the canvas.

Bess had been proud of her painting.

But now, as she picked up her paintbrush, it struck her as boring. *So ordinary,* she thought. *So . . . fairyish.*

Her thoughts strayed to Gabby's description of the wedding. "Now, that would be an exciting painting," Bess said to herself.

"What's that?" asked Prilla as she flew by.

"I was just thinking about Gabby's wedding," said Bess.

"That's funny. So was I," said Prilla.

"I was thinking I might make a painting of it," Bess said.

"Oh, Bess, you should. That would be almost as good as being there," Prilla said. Bess's paintings were magical that way.

Bess took out the pencil she kept tucked behind her ear. She began to make a sketch on a little piece of birch bark. She drew two Clumsies as tall as palm trees—all Clumsies looked like giants to Bess. But then her imagination failed her.

"What are their clothes made from? The Clumsies, I mean," Bess wondered. "A fairy gown would be sewn from lily petals, or maybe a rose. But that would never fit a Clumsy."

"I don't know," Prilla replied. "I've never thought about where Clumsies get their clothes."

"Speaking of flowers, what do the Clumsies do with them?" Bess asked. "Clumsies are too big to rest in a magnolia when they get tired of dancing. And how do they dance without wings, anyway? Their feet would never leave the ground! What kind of dancing is that?"

"They must look very silly," Prilla agreed.

Bess glanced at her sketch and frowned. "You're lucky, Prilla," she said. "You could just blink over to the mainland and see the wedding for yourself." Prilla had the special ability to travel to the world of Clumsies by blinking. She was the only fairy in Pixie Hollow with that talent.

"I guess I could," Prilla said. "But we haven't been properly invited."

"Oh, right," said Bess.

"You could go, too. You could fly through the hole in the old fig tree to get to the girls' world," Prilla pointed out.

"I could," said Bess. "But like you said, we haven't been invited. Besides, I wouldn't know where to go when I got there."

"I suppose that's true," Prilla said.

The two were quiet for a moment, thinking their own thoughts.

"It *would* be fun to be a gnat on the wall, though, wouldn't it?" Bess murmured. "Just to see the wedding, without anyone knowing you're there?"

Prilla said something in reply, but Bess wasn't listening. She was gazing off in the direction of Havendish Stream—and the old fig tree.

chapter 2

The next morning, Gabby stood in the doorway of her bedroom. Her pink flower girl dress was zipped up and buttoned. Her hair was brushed, her shoes were buckled, and her wings were on straight. She was ready for her big day.

But where was everyone else?

Gabby tiptoed across the hall to Mia's room and peeked in. Mia stood before the mirror, brushing her long hair. Lainey sat on the bed, and Kate was fidgeting with her skirt.

"I still don't understand why I have to dress up," Kate grumbled. "Julia's the one getting married. Not me."

Mia turned from the mirror. "You just don't like wearing dresses because they show your knees," she pointed out.

Kate looked down at her knees. They were covered with scrapes from soccer and softball and many adventures in Never Land. She frowned and tugged the hem of her skirt lower. "I don't like wearing dresses, period. You can't climb trees in a dress."

"You *could*," Lainey pointed out. "But someone might see your underwear."

"Exactly!" cried Kate.

"No one is going to be climbing trees today," said Mia. "It's a wedding! Anyway, I *like* getting dressed up." She picked up a flowered barrette and clipped it in her hair.

As she admired herself in the mirror, Mia caught sight of Gabby peeping in the door. Mia sighed. "Will you ever learn to knock?" she asked.

Gabby knocked, then stepped into the room.

"Gabby, you look very nice," said Lainey.

"Just like a flower fairy," Kate agreed. "Too bad the fairies can't see you."

Gabby cast a worried glance at her sister. Would she tell Kate and Lainey about her visit to Pixie Hollow?

Mia frowned but didn't say anything.

"Are we leaving soon?" Gabby asked.

"I don't know," Mia replied. "Go find Mami and ask her."

Gabby sighed and wandered down the hall to her parents' room. She stood in the doorway. Her parents were rushing around getting ready.

"Have you seen my green tie?" Gabby's father called. He still had a blob of shaving cream under his chin.

"Look in the closet," Gabby's mother said. "Now, where did I leave my purse?" She brushed past Gabby, trailing perfume.

"When are we leaving?" Gabby asked.

"Soon," her mother promised.

Gabby went back down the hall, scuffing her feet. She hated waiting. It seemed as if they would never get to the wedding!

At the end of the hall was a small window that overlooked the backyard. Gabby pressed her nose to the glass, gazing at the garden below. She could see the flower bed where she'd first met Prilla.

Was something moving among the marigolds? Gabby squinted. She thought she saw a flash of golden light among the orange and red flowers.

"All ready to go?" asked her father.

Gabby whirled around. Her parents, along with Mia, Kate, and Lainey, were in the hallway. "What are you looking at?" her father asked, coming to stand by her.

"Nothing, Papi. Just Bingo," Gabby said, referring to the family cat. Quickly, she stepped away from the window.

"Oh, sweetie," said her mother, looking at her closely for the first time. "You can't wear those to the wedding."

Gabby glanced down at her clothes. She wondered what her mother meant. Was there something wrong with her dress or her shoes?

"Julia is expecting a flower girl, not a fairy. You'll have to leave your wings at home," said her mother.

She might as well have asked Gabby to leave her arms at home. "Mami, no!" Gabby cried, clutching the straps on her shoulders.

Her mother knelt down next to her. "I know you love your wings," she said. "But this is Julia's special day. Can you do it for her?"

Gabby looked over at Mia, Kate, and

Lainey. Mia gave her a tiny nod, as if to say, "You can do it."

Gabby turned back to her mother. "Okay," she agreed with a sigh.

Slowly, she slipped one arm out of the straps, then the other. Her back felt bare where the wings had been. "I'm going to put them away," she said.

In her room, Gabby carefully folded her wings and placed them on the bed. She didn't feel quite as excited as she had before. Without her wings, being a flower girl lost some of its magic.

Gabby heard a tiny rattle behind her, like a key turning in a lock. She looked around. The sound had come from her closet.

Gabby watched as a teeny head poked out of the keyhole. Two small arms emerged next. After a bit of wriggling, a pair of iridescent wings followed.

The fairy flew into the room. She had a long, messy ponytail and a smudge of paint on her cheek. It was Bess.

When Bess saw Gabby, her face lit up. "You're here! So I'm not too late!"

"Too late for what?" asked Gabby.

"The wedding, of course!" Bess said. "I'd like to come with you. If you don't mind, that is."

Gabby's heart lifted. A fairy had come to see her in the wedding! Her excitement returned. "Yay! But— Oh!" Suddenly, Gabby remembered her promise to Mia.

"What's wrong?" Bess asked.

If Gabby told Bess what Mia had said,

the fairy might decide to go home.

I promised Mia I wouldn't say anything about fairies or Pixie Hollow, Gabby thought. *But I never said I wouldn't* bring *a fairy.*

"You can come," she told Bess at last. "But you can't let anyone see you."

"That's all right. I can hide in your basket," Bess said. She flew into the flower basket. Gabby covered her with a tissue

from a box next to her bed. And not a moment too soon, for just then they heard a knock on the door.

Mia, Kate, and Lainey walked in. "Are you okay, Gabby?" Lainey asked.

Gabby stood up straight. "I am now."

"Mami and Papi say we'll be late if we don't leave right away." Mia's eyes darted to the closet door. "You didn't go to Never Land, did you?" she whispered.

"Of course not," Gabby said. And squeezing past Mia and the other girls, she headed for the stairs.

Chapter 3

City Park was the biggest park in town. It had a duck pond, a carousel, and a little grassy hill where people went to fly kites. There were lots of paths for walking or riding bikes and benches where you could sit and rest in the shade.

The wedding was taking place near the pond, which was ringed with giant willow trees. Gabby saw rows and rows of white chairs facing the water. A great white tent had been set up on the grass. A few people

scurried around inside it, laying silver-
ware on tables and putting out food.

"Isn't this a lovely place for a wedding!"
her mother said.

Gabby swallowed hard. It all looked
much bigger and more grown-up than she
had imagined—big, and a little scary. She
wriggled her shoulders, feeling the empty
space on her back where her wings should
have been.

Bess poked her head out from Gabby's
basket. "Are we there yet?"

"Not now, Bess," Gabby whispered. She
pulled the tissue back over the fairy, just
as Lainey walked up next to her. Lainey
had her sweater bundled in her arms, as if
she were carrying a package.

"Are you sure you're okay? About your
wings, I mean," she said.

Gabby nodded. She held her hand over the basket so Lainey couldn't peek inside.

"We'd better find someone and let them know we're here," Mrs. Vasquez said.

At that moment, a woman in a pink suit came striding toward them. She carried a clipboard in the crook of her elbow. "Is this our flower girl?" she exclaimed. She checked her clipboard, adding, "Gabriela Vasquez?"

"It's Gabby, not Gabriela," Gabby said shyly.

"Aren't you cute," the woman replied. She made a little checkmark on her clipboard, then turned to Gabby's parents. "I'm Amanda Cork, the wedding planner. I'm here to make sure everything is perfect."

"Can we go say hi to Julia?" Mia asked.

"Of course not!" the wedding planner exclaimed. "A bride should never be disturbed when she's dressing for her big day—"

"Is that Mia and Gabby I hear?" a familiar voice called. "And Lainey and Kate?"

The girls turned. Not far from the pond was a little building known as the clubhouse. Julia's smiling face peeked out of the door.

"Julia!" the girls cried, rushing to her.

When Gabby saw her babysitter, her mouth opened in surprise. Instead of her usual jeans and T-shirt, Julia was dressed in a long gown made of white lace.

"You look like a princess!" Gabby exclaimed.

"You look really pretty," Lainey agreed.

"I love your dress," Mia gushed.

"Yeah, it really covers your knees," added Kate.

Julia laughed. "Thank you," she said. "You all look very nice, too."

Ms. Cork hurried up behind them. "Are these girls bothering you?" she asked.

"Of course not," said Julia. "They were just saying hello."

"There's time for all that later." Ms. Cork sniffed. "The wedding starts in"— she checked her watch—"fifty-six minutes. You should finish getting ready! I'm sure you girls can find some way to amuse yourselves. Not you, Gabby," the wedding planner added as the girls started to walk away. "You can stay. I have some flower girl instructions to give you."

As the other girls left, Gabby looked around the clubhouse. Inside was a cozy room with a sofa, a dressing table, and a full-length mirror.

Gabby pointed to a long piece of gauzy fabric draped over a hanger on the closet door. "What's that?"

"That's my veil," Julia replied. "Isn't it pretty?"

Gabby nodded. The veil cascaded in lovely, loose folds. It reminded her of a waterfall. She wondered how it felt—

"No touching!" Ms. Cork exclaimed. "Your hands might be dirty."

Gabby jerked her hand away. "They aren't dirty," she said, but she clasped her hands behind her back anyway.

Gabby waited for her flower girl

instructions. But the wedding planner started talking to Julia. Something about place mats—or was it place cards? Gabby was having trouble following the conversation.

Suddenly, she realized Julia and Ms. Cork were heading for the door. "Wait here, Gabby. We'll be right back," Julia said. The door closed behind them.

As soon as they were gone, Bess fluttered out of Gabby's basket. "I thought they'd never leave! I'm going outside to look around."

"Are you going far?" Gabby asked, worried. She was a little scared of Ms. Cork, and she didn't want to be left alone. "Don't you want to see me be a flower girl?"

"I do!" Bess said. "I just want to take a

peek. I'll be back in a firefly's flash." With a little wave, Bess flew out the window.

Gabby sighed. As she waited for Julia and Ms. Cork to return, her eyes wandered around the room. But they kept coming back to the long white veil.

The filmy fabric looked a bit like her own fairy wings. It looked . . . magical. Gabby reached out a finger and stroked the veil, forgetting that she wasn't supposed to touch it.

As she ran her finger along the edges, the veil suddenly slid off the hanger. It landed in a heap at her feet. Gabby gasped. She glanced around to make sure no one had seen, then quickly gathered up the fabric.

She meant to put it right back. But once the veil was in her arms, Gabby couldn't resist the urge to try it on.

Just for a second, she told herself. *No one will know.*

Gabby tried to put the veil on her head, but it kept sliding back to the floor. At last she discovered two little combs attached to the corners. She pushed the combs into her hair and pretended she was walking down the aisle.

But the veil was too long. She kept tripping over the end.

"Oopsie!" Gabby said as she stepped on it once, then again. "Whoops!"

At last, by wadding the trailing veil into a ball, Gabby managed to carry it over to the mirror. But when she let the veil flow down, it didn't look pretty or princessy anymore. Instead of falling in long, lovely folds, the fabric was wrinkly and crumpled. There was a smudgy mark in one corner. Looking closer, Gabby saw that it was a footprint.

A sick, scared feeling churned in her stomach. *Maybe if I hurry and put it back, no one will notice anything is wrong,* she thought.

But Gabby had another problem. She couldn't reach the hanger. It was too high over her head.

Where's Bess? Gabby thought. *She could use magic to put it back— Oh!*

Suddenly, she remembered the thimbleful of fairy dust in her pocket. Gabby knew fairy dust could make things fly and float. Maybe it could lift the veil for her.

Gabby pulled out the thimble and sprinkled some dust on the veil. "Abracadabra," she said, for good measure. "Go back to your hanger."

At first, nothing happened. Then, slowly, the veil rose into the air. Gabby sighed with relief.

But the veil kept on rising. It floated past Gabby, past the hanger, and headed for the open window.

The veil flapped like the wings of a great white bird, then soared outside and disappeared.

Chapter 4

Bess hovered beneath the canopy of the big white tent. Below her, Clumsies were briskly preparing for the celebration. They were setting tables, folding napkins, and carrying platters of food.

Bess marveled at the scene. The round tables reminded her of the tables in the Home Tree dining room—except they were built for giants!

She swooped down to look at one of the place settings. The bowl was big enough for her to bathe in. The teaspoon was the size of a garden fairy's shovel. Fifteen fairies could sit comfortably around the dinner plate.

Bess darted out of the way as a Clumsy set down a vase filled with flowers. She didn't worry about being spotted. Most grown-ups didn't believe in fairies, and fairies could only be seen by Clumsies who believed. But she did need to take care not to get squashed.

When the Clumsy was gone, Bess poked around the flower arrangement. She undid an artfully folded napkin to see how it was done. She made faces at her reflection in a soup spoon. *How am I ever going to decide what to put into my painting?* she wondered. There was so much to look at—and everything was huge! She'd need a canvas the size of the Home Tree to fit it all in.

Bess held up her thumb and forefinger. She looked through the window they made, trying to frame the scene in her mind.

Bess gasped. Through the makeshift frame, she saw two tiny figures on the other side of the tent. They looked like fairies!

"Fly with you!" Bess swooped toward them, calling out the fairy greeting.

The fairies didn't respond. They didn't even move. As she landed, Bess saw they weren't fairies at all, but little statues of a man and woman.

Bess walked around the statues, studying them. The woman wore a white dress, and the man was in a dark suit. The carved faces were blank and expressionless. Bess couldn't imagine what they were for.

I'll have to ask Gabby, she thought. As a matter of fact, it was time she found her friend.

But as she fluttered her wings to leave, Bess found that her feet were stuck. She was sinking into the ground, which, actually, was not ground at all but—

"Frosting!" Bess exclaimed. She was up to her ankles in it. Now she realized that she was standing on a giant cake. Her tiny footprints covered the top tier.

"Oh, smudge!" cried Bess. She tried to swipe one of the footprints away with her paintbrush. But she only made a bigger smear. "Double smudge!"

Maybe I can turn the footprints into a pattern, she thought. *That way they'll look like they're there on purpose.*

Bess began to walk around the top of the cake, weaving in and out. It was slow going. The frosting was as thick and heavy as mud. It took effort to drag each foot out. But at last she managed to create a beautiful spiral pattern around the statues.

She stepped back to admire her work. "Not bad, if I do say so my— Ahhh!"

The edge of cake she'd been standing on gave way suddenly. Bess slid down in an avalanche of frosting. She bounced off the second tier, rolled to the first, then fell onto the table.

She groaned and sat up. Looking back

at the cake, she saw a Bess-sized track running down the side.

"Blasted broken brushes! How am I going to fix *that*?" she exclaimed.

But before she could even think of fixing the cake, she needed to get cleaned up. She was sticky with frosting.

Somewhere nearby, Bess could hear the sound of water trickling. She flew toward it, hoping to find a place to wash.

Bess followed the sound to a table. There were bowls piled high with strawberries, and right in the middle was a giant fountain. It flowed with something thick, brown, and sweet-smelling.

"Chocolate!" Bess exclaimed. She had found the chocolate waterfall!

Bess hesitated. She really needed to get cleaned up. But if there was one thing

Bess loved almost as much as painting, it was chocolate.

"I'll just take a teensy taste," she told herself. "Then I'll be on my way." Bess climbed onto the edge of the fountain.

At that moment, a Clumsy set a bowl of strawberries down right next to her. Startled, Bess lost her balance—

Sploosh! She fell up to her waist into the chocolate.

"Ugh!" Bess stood on her tiptoes, trying to hold her wings above the thick brown liquid. If they went under, she'd never get out!

She tried to lift her legs. *Gloop.* The chocolate pulled one of her shoes right off.

Bess reached into the chocolate. She stuck her arm in all the way up to the elbow. But she couldn't find her shoe. She tried with her other arm. She thought she felt it with the tip of her finger. She stretched her arms as far as she could until she finally grabbed hold of the shoe.

Bess stood up with a gasp, wiping chocolate from her chin. She was covered from neck to toe. Luckily, she'd managed to keep her wings dry. Now she fluttered them hard to pull herself out.

She landed on the table, making a big chocolate splatter.

"Ugh! What a mess!" How was she going to clean herself up now?

A loud scream made her jump. "That's the biggest bug I've ever seen!" a Clumsy exclaimed.

"It's horrible!" said another.

Bess glanced around nervously, looking for the big, horrible bug. Instead, she saw two Clumsies holding covered platters. They were both staring down at her.

They can't be looking at me, Bess thought. *Grown-up Clumsies can't see fairies, unless . . . Uh-oh!*

Bess suddenly realized they *could* see her. Covered in chocolate, she was no longer invisible. Now she looked like a big, ugly brown bug!

"Squish it!" one of the Clumsies said. The next thing Bess saw was a huge silver lid coming toward her.

Chapter 5

Outside, Gabby hurried across the grass toward the rows of white chairs. Guests had started to arrive. The seats were beginning to fill with people.

"Bess?" Gabby whispered. She crept along the aisle. She peeked under the chairs, but all she saw were feet. Where could the fairy be?

"What are you looking for?" asked a voice behind her.

Gabby jumped and spun around. A boy her age was standing there. He was dressed in a little blue suit with a white bow tie. In his hands, he held a small satin pillow.

"I was trying to find my friend," Gabby said, staring at the pillow. She wondered what it was for. Was the boy planning to take a nap?

"Why were you looking under the chairs?" the boy asked.

Gabby remembered her promise to Mia about not mentioning fairies. "I thought I saw a butterfly," she fibbed.

"I caught a butterfly yesterday," the boy said. "It was yellow and blue. I put it in my bug hotel."

"What's a bug hotel?" Gabby asked.

"It's this jar with holes in the lid. When you catch a bug, you put it in there. The bug can have a drink of water and some leaves to eat. Maybe it can take a nap. Then you have to let the bug go, so it can go home to its family."

"Can I see it?" Gabby asked.

The boy shrugged. "Nah. It's at home."

Gabby hoped the boy would go away now. How could she find Bess with him standing right there?

A hand suddenly clamped down on her shoulder. "There you are, Gabriela!" Ms. Cork exclaimed. "I've been looking all over for you."

Fear seized Gabby. Had Ms. Cork found out what she'd done?

But the wedding planner didn't look

angry. She held up a little box. "These are your rose petals," she said, emptying the contents into Gabby's basket. "You're to sprinkle them when you walk down the aisle. Can you do that?"

Gabby nodded, clutching the basket. She hoped Ms. Cork would leave now, too, so she could go back to looking for the veil and Bess.

But Ms. Cork seemed to be in no hurry. "Let's practice," she said. "Take a handful of petals and sprinkle them. Sprinkle them *gaily*!"

Gabby lobbed a fistful of petals into the air. Most of them landed on Ms. Cork's feet.

"A little less force next time," she said, shaking off her shoes. "I see you've met Daniel. He's our ring bearer. He'll be

going down the aisle right in front of you, so all you have to do is follow him. Can you do that?"

Gabby nodded again. She wished Ms. Cork would stop talking to her as if she were a baby.

At that moment, a shout came from the tent, followed by a loud clatter.

Ms. Cork frowned. "I'd better go see what that's about," she said, to Gabby's relief. "Don't go running off anywhere. The wedding will be starting very soon." She bustled away.

"I don't like her," said Daniel.

"Me either," said Gabby. "Okay, I'll see you later—"

"Wait," said Daniel. "I want to show you something."

He led Gabby over to a row of white chairs. Tucked beneath one of the chairs was a beautiful kite.

"It's nice," said Gabby. The kite was shaped like a dragonfly, with purple wings and big green eyes.

"Dragonflies are my favorite bugs," he said. "My mom and dad said we can go fly

the kite as soon as the wedding is over. You can come if you want."

"Okay," said Gabby. She was starting to think Daniel was nice.

Just then, she saw something over Daniel's shoulder that made her heart pound. The veil was drifting across the lawn. It floated past like a ghost. Then it disappeared around the side of the tent.

Gabby knew there was no time to find Bess now. She'd have to catch the veil herself!

As she ran after it, she heard Daniel call, "Hey, where are you going?"

Behind the tent, the veil was rolling across the grass like a big white tumbleweed. She tried to catch it, but it was always just out of reach.

Then the veil became snagged on a

bush. Gabby lunged for it. But as her fingertips brushed the fabric, a gust of wind snatched the veil away. It soared up . . . up . . . up. One end flapped, as if waving good-bye.

Gabby collapsed onto the grass. She blinked back tears of frustration. She was never going to be fast enough to catch a magical flying veil. Unless . . .

Gabby reached into her pocket and found the thimble bucket. There was still a tiny bit of fairy dust clinging to the sides. Maybe it was enough.

Gabby had only had one flying lesson in Pixie Hollow. She tried to remember how it worked. *Think happy thoughts and kick your feet*—that was it, wasn't it? Or were you *not* supposed to kick?

There wasn't time to waste. She'd have

to figure it out as she went. She sprinkled the remaining dust over herself.

Gabby felt a tingly feeling, like bubbles rising in a soda bottle. The next thing she knew, her feet were lifting off the ground.

Chapter 6

Not far away, on the buffet table, Bess was running for her life.

Wham! A massive serving spoon crashed down. It missed her by a hair. Bess changed direction in time to see a fist holding a crumpled napkin swing toward her.

With a flutter of wings, Bess dodged it. She zigzagged across the table, searching for an exit.

If only she could fly! But the Clumsies were always just above her, blocking her way. They filled the air with their shouts and their flailing arms. Bess couldn't find a clear space for takeoff.

She scurried between two platters of fruit. It was becoming tougher and tougher to run. The chocolate that covered her was hardening. It formed a thick brown shell over her whole body. Her hands felt like they were inside chocolate mittens. Chocolate boots encased her feet.

Slam! A hand swung at her, upending a bowl of fruit. Strawberries tumbled everywhere. In the space where the bowl had been, Bess saw an opening. She ran toward it, jumping over berries that rolled into her path.

As she reached the edge of the table, a Clumsy loomed over her. He held two platter lids in his hands. He clashed the

lids together like cymbals just as Bess leaped.

She felt the lids whoosh past her—so close they grazed the tips of her wings. A second later, she tumbled into the grass below.

Bess didn't waste a moment. She fluttered her wings and flew away. She had to find Gabby!

Outside the tent, Bess looked around.

She spotted the small building where she'd left the little girl.

The door was shut tight, but Bess flew up to the window. She clung to the sill, peeking in. Julia, the girls' babysitter, was talking to another Clumsy.

"I don't know what could have happened to it," Julia was saying.

"Well, it must be around here somewhere. Veils don't just fly away on their own," the woman replied.

Bess looked all around the room. There was no sign of Gabby. She started to turn from the window.

Suddenly, two hands closed around her. "Gotcha!" someone cried.

Bess fluttered and fought, trying to free herself. But the hands cupped her, holding tight. Through the cracks between the Clumsy's fingers, an eyeball peeped in at her.

"Ooh! What kind of bug are you?" said a boy's voice.

"I'm not a bug!" Bess cried. If the boy heard her, he gave no sign. He shoved Bess into a little paper bag and closed it.

"Let me out!" Bess kicked at the side of the bag.

"Are you hungry, bug? Here are some leaves to eat." The boy opened the bag and thrust a leaf down at Bess. "When we get home you can have lots more."

The bag closed again. Curled in her tiny prison, Bess sighed. She thought about how she'd ended up in this spot. *Why didn't I just stay in Gabby's basket?* she asked herself.

She thought of Gabby in her pink dress. She'd been so excited for Bess to watch her in the wedding. Surely she was wondering where Bess was.

She probably thinks I forgot all about her, Bess thought miserably. *And what's going to happen to me now?*

Bess realized she hadn't been completely honest with Gabby. Of course she'd wanted to see Gabby be a flower girl. But she'd been more concerned about making her painting.

Bess's stomach rumbled, as if it, too, were sorry to find itself in such a fix. She *was* hungry. She hadn't had a thing to eat since she left Pixie Hollow.

Bess looked down at her chocolate-covered hands, her chocolate-covered arms, and her chocolate-covered legs. There was nothing she could do about Gabby right now. But there was one thing she *could* do.

She broke off a bit of chocolate and began to nibble.

Chapter 7

"Is it time yet?" asked Kate.

Mia, Kate, and Lainey were lingering near the rows of white chairs. In the half hour since they'd left Gabby with Julia, they'd walked all the way around the pond—twice. They'd made bets on the flavor of wedding cake. (Kate guessed chocolate. Lainey guessed vanilla. Mia guessed lemon with raspberry cream.) They'd even hidden beneath one of the big willow trees to spy on guests as they arrived. They had run out of ideas for things to do, and *still* the wedding hadn't begun.

Lainey shifted her bundled sweater to her other arm, then checked her watch. "The wedding doesn't start for another twenty minutes," she said.

"Why are you carrying your sweater around like that? Why don't you put it on?" Kate asked irritably. Boredom always made her cranky.

Lainey tucked the sweater more firmly under her arm. "I'm not cold," she replied with a shrug.

"Let's go sit down," Mia suggested. "Look, there are Mami and Papi. We can sit next to them."

"Where do you think Gabby is?" Lainey

asked as they made their way over to the seats.

"Having fun with Julia, probably," Mia replied. Her brow furrowed. "It's just not fair."

"What's not fair?" asked Kate.

"I always wanted to be a flower girl, but I never got the chance," Mia said. "And now I'm too old. It doesn't seem fair that Gabby gets to be one. Isn't the point of being a big sister getting to do everything first?"

"I think you would have been a great flower girl," Lainey said.

"I know." Mia sighed.

"Oh!" Lainey gasped and stood up from her chair.

"What is it?" asked Kate.

"I saw a fairy! There, by the bushes," Lainey whispered.

The other girls looked to where she was pointing. "I don't see anything. Are you sure?" Mia asked.

"Yes . . . well, no. Not completely sure," Lainey replied. "I only saw a flash, but it looked like a fairy."

"What would a fairy be doing here?" Kate asked.

Mia bit her lip. "You don't suppose they would have followed us, do you?"

"Nah," said Kate. "Why would they come without telling us?"

"I guess you're right," Mia said, relaxing a little. "Maybe you just imagined it, Lainey."

"I wouldn't mind if it was a fairy, though," Kate added. "It would be more exciting than all of this waiting around. In fact, I wish we were in Pixie Hollow right now!"

"Kate! Shh! Not so loud," Mia whispered. She glanced over at her parents to see if they'd heard. But they were busy chatting with some other wedding guests.

At that moment, she saw a flash of pink out of the corner of her eye. Something was rising over the top of the tent.

Mia gasped. It was Gabby! The little girl was floating through the air like a lost balloon.

Mia opened her mouth to shout, then thought better of it. She jerked back around and stared straight ahead, trying to think what to do.

"What's wrong?" asked Kate.

"Don't look now," Mia muttered.

Of course, that only made Kate and Lainey want to look. They twisted around in their seats.

"Holy guacamole!" said Kate.

"I said not to look," Mia hissed. But she had turned around again, too.

Gabby paddled the air, as if she were swimming. One hand still clutched her little basket. Her legs kicked helplessly behind her.

She drifted over a crowd of wedding guests who were standing on the grass in front of the tent. None of them noticed the little girl above their heads.

"Don't look up. Don't look up," Mia pleaded.

Then Gabby started to sink. She was headed right for a woman's large sunhat.

"She's going to crash!" Kate cried.

Lainey put her hands over her glasses. "I can't watch."

At the last second, Gabby paddled back up through the air. Mia, Kate, and Lainey watched as she sailed over the trees around the pond and disappeared from view.

The girls exchanged glances. Mia turned to her mother. In the calmest voice she could manage, she said, "Mami, we'll be right back."

"Where are you going?" her mother asked in surprise. "The ceremony is about to start."

"I have to go to the bathroom," Mia told her.

Her mother sighed. "All right. But hurry back."

The girls sprang from their chairs and raced in the direction Gabby had gone.

Down by the pond, it was shady and quiet. A light breeze stirred the leaves of the willow trees.

"I don't see her," Lainey whispered as they walked around the edge of the pond. The girls kept their voices low so none of the other wedding guests would hear.

"I can't believe Gabby was flying!" Kate said. She began to giggle.

Lainey started to giggle, too. "And at Julia's wedding!"

Mia frowned. "It's not funny, you guys. Remember the first time we flew in Pixie Hollow? We all ended up in the stream."

The girls looked at the lily-covered pond. "You don't think Gabby fell in, do you?" asked Lainey.

"No. We would have heard the splash," said Kate.

"Look!" Mia pointed at a nearby willow. Its leaves were trembling violently. Tipping their heads back, the girls could see Gabby high in the branches.

"Gabby!" Mia said in her loudest whisper. "Get down from there *right now!*"

Gabby didn't respond. She was thrashing around in the leaves. The girls could see something long and white tangled in the branches.

"What's she doing?" Lainey asked.

"Do you hear me, Gabby?" Mia said. "You'd better come down now, or else."

"I can't," Gabby replied. Her voice sounded small and scared.

"Why don't you fly down?" Mia asked.

"I can't let go." Gabby peered through the leaves at them. She was clinging to a branch with one hand, as if to keep from blowing away. Her arm held tight to her flower girl basket, and her other hand clutched a piece of long white fabric. The veil fluttered as if it were being blown by a breeze.

"I think she's stuck," said Kate.

"I *told* her no magic at the wedding," Mia said. "She never listens!"

"We can't leave her up there," Lainey said.

"I know." Mia turned to Kate. "Remember what I said about no one climbing trees at the wedding?"

"Yeah," said Kate.

"Well," Mia said, "I take it back."

Chapter 8

"Can you see anybody coming?" asked Kate as she scrambled up onto a low branch of the willow.

"All clear," said Lainey, who was standing lookout.

"Good," Kate said, climbing higher. "I don't want anyone to see my underwear."

Mia was standing beneath the tree, holding out her arms in case someone fell. "No one is going to care about your underwear if we get caught," she explained.

"All the same, I wish I'd worn pants," said Kate. She pulled herself onto another branch with ease.

When she reached the branch where Gabby was clinging, Kate inched out as far as she could. "Give me your hand."

Gabby shook her head.

"Don't be scared," said Kate. "Just let go of that curtain, or whatever it is."

Gabby shook her head again, harder this time.

"Well, you're going to have to fly down. Do you have any more fairy dust?" Kate asked. "Then we could both fly down together!"

"I used it all up," Gabby said.

"It figures," Kate said with a sigh. "I'll

guide you, then. I'll need both hands to climb, so hold on to my shirt."

Gabby let go of the tree branch and took hold of the back of Kate's shirt. Kate began to climb down, pulling Gabby along with her. "Stop kicking, Gabby. You're throwing me off balance," she complained.

"I'm not doing anything," Gabby said.

"Then what's wiggling?" Kate asked.

It was the veil, of course. It had begun to flap again. Just as Kate reached the lowest branch, it broke free of Gabby's grasp and sailed into the air. The force of it tugged Gabby and Kate out of the tree.

Gabby landed on Kate, Kate landed on Mia, and Mia landed on the ground. Gabby's basket rolled away. The rose petals scattered.

"My petals!" Gabby wailed. All the tears she'd been holding back since losing the veil flooded her eyes.

The other girls gathered around her. Lainey gave the little girl's shoulder a comforting pat. "They're only flower petals, Gabby," she said. "At least no one got hurt."

"Not *very* hurt, anyway." Mia rubbed her bruised backside.

"I wish I was never a flower girl!" Gabby sobbed. "Ms. Cork is going to be mad about the petals. And Julia is going to be mad when she finds out I lost her veil—"

Mia raised a hand. "Hold on. Did you just say you *lost* Julia's veil?"

"Maybe you'd better explain," said Kate.

So Gabby told them everything, from her sneaky-quick visit to Pixie Hollow to bringing Bess to the wedding in her flower basket to losing the veil out of Julia's dressing-room window. By the time she was done explaining, Gabby's tears had dried. In truth, it felt good to finally tell someone else about everything that had gone wrong.

To Gabby's relief, Kate and Lainey weren't mad about her breaking their Pixie Hollow rule. And when she heard about Bess, Mia only rubbed her forehead and said, "Oh, Gabby."

"I *knew* I saw a fairy!" Lainey exclaimed.

"What am I going to do?" Gabby asked. "I lost the veil *and* Bess."

"We'll help you get the veil back," Mia said. "As for Bess, I'm sure she's wondering where you are right now. The wedding is going to start any minute."

"How are we going to get all the way up there?" Lainey asked. They could see the veil flying over the meadow, swooping among the kites in the sky.

"Gabby could fly," Kate suggested. "Although she's not so great at steering."

"We can't risk it. What if someone saw her?" said Mia.

Gabby gazed toward the colorful kites. "I have an idea!" she said.

*

A few minutes later, Gabby was high up in the sky. She could see the whole park stretched out below her—the ball fields, the carousel, the pond, and the big white tent.

How much fun it was to fly! Clinging to Daniel's kite, Gabby turned a little loop. She was using the kite to hide behind. Anyone passing by would think the other girls were just out having fun on a sunny summer day.

The girls had found the kite in Daniel's hiding spot. Gabby had wanted to ask if she

could borrow it, but she didn't know where Daniel was and there wasn't a moment to lose. She hoped he wouldn't mind that she got to fly his kite before he did.

A sharp tug on the kite string made Gabby look down. On the ground below, she saw Mia making a "hurry up" gesture.

The veil was just ahead of Gabby. It turned a loop-de-loop in the wind. Gabby steered the kite toward it. The veil dodged right. Gabby followed on the kite. The veil zoomed down. Gabby stayed on its tail.

At last, it was within reach. Gabby snatched up an edge of the fabric. As soon as she had it, Kate began to reel her in. Gabby landed with the veil clasped in her arms.

"You did it!" Mia exclaimed, giving her a hug.

Faint music floated from the direction of the pond. Lainey checked her watch. "It's almost noon! The wedding must be starting!"

"If we run, we can get this to Julia just in time," Kate said.

Only then did they take a good look at the veil. The fabric was rumpled and torn in one place. There were grass stains from the veil's tumble across the lawn. A few feathers clung to it, picked up from who knows where.

"There's no way we can give it to her like this!" Mia said.

"But there's no time left to fix it," Lainey said.

The tears welled up in Gabby's eyes again. Everything had gone wrong. She had spoiled Julia's perfect wedding. Worse than thinking about the trouble she'd be in was knowing how disappointed Julia would be.

Chapter 9

The music woke Bess. At first, she didn't know where she was. Then she spotted the brown walls of her paper-bag prison. Her stomach ached and her wings felt cramped.

Bess wiggled her fingers and toes to wake them up. She was surprised to find they moved freely. Where had her chocolate mittens gone?

Ugh, Bess thought. She'd eaten the chocolate—every last bit of it. That explained her stomachache.

The bag shook. Bess heard the boy shout, "Hey, that's *my* kite! What the— Oh my gosh!"

The bag suddenly dropped from his grasp. Bess couldn't flap her wings in time to stop herself from falling. She grunted as the bag landed in the grass. Bright light flooded in.

She could escape!

Bess dove toward the opening. As she fluttered out of the bag, she came face to face with the boy. When he saw her, his mouth opened so wide Bess could have climbed right inside it.

"A fairy!"

Before he could catch her again, Bess zipped away. She searched for a place to hide.

"Bess, up here!" a familiar voice called.

Bess looked up—and almost fell out of the air in shock. Her friends from Pixie Hollow were standing on the clubhouse roof. Prilla, Tink, Rosetta, and Dulcie were there, along with several other fairies.

"What are you doing here?" asked Rosetta.

"What are *you* doing here?" Bess replied in amazement.

"I came on a blink," Prilla replied. "I thought I'd just watch the wedding in secret, like you and I talked about. But then I saw the trouble. So I went back and brought everyone along to help."

Bess smiled at her friends. "You mean, you all came to rescue me?"

"Actually, no," Prilla said in surprise. "I didn't even know you were here. I meant Gabby. She's in trouble. We have to help her!"

*

When the fairies spotted the girls, they were trudging back toward the clubhouse. They held the ruined veil between them.

Bess overheard Gabby say, "What am I going to tell Julia?"

"Tell her you were playing with her veil when you shouldn't have been," Mia replied. "That's the truth."

"What's that fluttering sound?" asked Lainey.

The girls looked up as the fairies swooped toward them. When she saw all her Pixie Hollow friends, Gabby cried, "You came!"

"Everyone wanted to see you be a flower girl," Bess said.

Gabby's face fell. "Julia won't want me to be in her wedding. Not when she finds out what I did to her veil."

"That's why we're here," said Prilla. "Hand it over!"

Gabby did, and at once fairies set about fixing the veil. A sewing-talent fairy named Hem stitched up the tear. Her needle darted in and out so quickly it was a silver blur. A cleaning-talent fairy worked a bit of magic on the stains. Silvermist, a water-talent fairy, added dewdrops so the veil sparkled in the sunlight.

Meanwhile, the flower-talent fairies hurried off to collect petals from around the park. They filled Gabby's basket to the brim.

When Bess showed Dulcie what she'd done to the wedding cake, Dulcie threw her hands up in horror. Then she and the other baking-talent fairies set to work patching it up. They hid the dents Bess had made in the frosting with little flowers they cut from strawberries.

In no time, everything was ready. The only thing left to do was to return the veil to Julia.

When Gabby knocked, the clubhouse door flew open right away. Julia stood in the doorway. "Did you find it?" she asked eagerly. "Oh, girls, I thought you were Ms. Cork. She's out looking for my veil. I don't know where it's gone."

While Julia's back was turned, Bess and the other fairies carried the veil in through the open window.

"That's terrible," said Lainey, stalling.

"What does it look like?" Kate asked.

Julia frowned. "It's long and white and it—well, it looks like a veil."

The fairies hung the veil on the hanger, then flew back out the window.

"You mean, like that?" Mia asked, pointing.

Julia turned just as the last fairy fluttered out. "Oh my gosh!" she exclaimed. "How did this get here?" She hurried over and lifted the veil from its hanger. "Want to help me put it on?" she asked the girls.

Of course they did. Kate and Mia helped fit the combs into Julia's hair, while Lainey and Gabby arranged the veil behind her.

"It looks different somehow," Julia said, examining herself in the mirror. "It's prettier than I remembered."

"You look even *better* than a princess," Gabby said.

Julia laughed. "I know it's just a piece of fabric. But something about it is special. Wearing a veil makes me *feel* like a bride. I guess that sounds silly, doesn't it?"

"No, it doesn't," said Gabby. "That's how I feel about my wings."

"Speaking of your wings, where *are* they?" asked Julia.

"Mami said I shouldn't wear them in the wedding," Gabby told her.

"But of course you can wear them!" Julia exclaimed. "They're part of what make you Gabby. Go put them on!"

If only she'd known sooner! "I can't," said Gabby. "They're at home."

"No, they're not," said Lainey. She unbundled the sweater she'd been carrying. There, to Gabby's amazement, were her beloved wings. "I took them from your room, just in case," Lainey explained. "It didn't seem right to leave them behind."

Gabby gave a little jump of joy. She slipped on the wings and sighed happily.

At that moment, Ms. Cork bustled into the room. "We can't wait any longer. The wedding should have started ten minutes ago! You'll have to get married without your— Oh, your veil!" she said when she saw Julia. "Where on earth did you find it?"

"It was right here after all," Julia said.

Ms. Cork gave a cluck of exasperation. Then she noticed the girls. "What are you all doing here? Hurry! Go find your seats! The wedding is starting!" She shooed Mia, Kate, and Lainey out of the room. "And Gabby, where did those wings come from? Take them off, please! It's time to start!"

"I told her she can wear them," Julia said. "I think they look perfect."

Ms. Cork threw up her hands. "Suit yourself. No one ever listens to the wedding planner." She hurried off, grumbling.

"Are you ready, Gabby?" Julia asked, taking her hand.

Gabby grinned and held up her flower girl basket. "I'm ready!"

(hapter 10

The ceremony went by in a joyful blur
for Gabby. Although Ms. Cork had told
her to walk down the aisle slowly, Gabby
skipped. She couldn't help it. She was so
happy, it took all her effort to keep from
floating away. When she thought no one
was looking, she gave a secret little wave
to the fairies, who were watching from a
tree branch.

In the end, Gabby forgot to use fairy

dust on the flower petals, but it didn't matter. None of the guests seemed to pay much attention to the petals on the ground. Their eyes were on Julia. The bride looked dazzling as she came down the aisle, her veil dancing on a breeze that no one else could feel.

Later, under the big white tent, there was food and music and dancing. Gabby laughed when Julia and her new husband cut the cake and dabbed frosting on each other's noses. The cake turned out to be lemon with vanilla cream, and all the older girls agreed that Mia had won the bet, her guess being the closest. They were allowed to choose their own slices. Gabby picked the biggest she could find, one with extra strawberry flowers.

As she carried it back to the table where the other girls were sitting, she heard grown-ups in the crowd talking.

". . . just adorable. Those fairy wings were the perfect touch."

"Such a happy little girl. She looked like she was walking on air."

". . . those tiny flowers on the cake. How did they ever make them?"

"Did you notice the little footprints on top, as if the cake toppers were dancing?"

". . . such a beautiful bride . . ."

". . . such an elegant bride . . ."

". . . such a graceful bride. And that veil! I've never seen one like it."

Gabby smiled to herself. None of the grown-ups, not even Julia, would ever know how truly special the veil was.

Then Gabby saw Daniel hurrying toward her. "Gabby," he said urgently. "I saw you. You were flying, weren't you?"

Gabby didn't want to lie. But she didn't want to break her promise to Mia, either. She took a big bite of cake so she wouldn't have to answer.

"Don't worry. I won't tell. Can you teach me to fly?" Daniel asked.

"Mmm," said Gabby, chewing.

Daniel lowered his voice. "I saw a fairy here," he whispered. "I caught her. But she got away."

Gabby considered. If Daniel had already seen the fairies, then they weren't a secret anymore. Besides, she'd borrowed his kite. She wanted to do something nice for him in return. "Want to meet her?" she said.

"The fairy? You know her?" Daniel looked stunned.

"It's okay," said Gabby. "She's my friend. Come on."

Gabby led Daniel to a small round table in the very back corner of the tent.

Mia, Kate, and Lainey were already there, eating cake. In the middle of the table was a plate with another slice of cake. A dozen fairies sat around it.

If any of the grown-ups at the wedding had bothered to look closer, they would have seen the cake disappearing in itty-bitty chunks, as if being picked away by invisible hands. But Gabby knew grown-ups never thought to look for such things.

"This cake is quite tasty," Dulcie was saying as Gabby and Daniel walked up. "Not as good as fairy cake, but not bad at all. Bess, you should try some!" she called over to the art fairy.

But Bess was busy painting. She had stretched out a napkin on the table to use as a canvas, anchoring it with salt and pepper shakers. She glanced over at

Dulcie and made a face. "I think I've had enough sweets for one day."

Just then, Bess froze. She'd spied Gabby and Daniel.

"Hey, everybody," Gabby said. "This is my friend. His name is Daniel."

Daniel stared at the fairies. His mouth hung open a little. "Say hi," Gabby whispered to him.

"Hi," Daniel echoed, finding his voice at last. "I'm . . . um . . . sorry I put you in a bag. I thought you were a bug," he told Bess.

"Well." Bess sniffed, then gave a little nod to show she accepted his apology.

Gabby moved around the table to look at Bess's painting. Here was the bride with her dancing veil. And here was the groom wearing a goofy grin and Gabby throwing petals and all the guests in their nice clothes. Bess had even painted the fairies, though they were so tiny they looked more like butterflies.

"Look, Daniel. There you are," Gabby said, pointing. Bess had painted Daniel holding his little pillow with the wedding rings and a serious expression on his face.

"What are you going to do with the painting when it's done?" asked Mia.

"I haven't really thought about it," said Bess, who never bothered to do much with her art after it was finished. For her, making the painting was the best part. "I guess I could take it back to Pixie Hollow. Or you could have it."

Gabby looked toward the center of the tent, where Julia and her new husband were dancing. As Julia twirled, her veil floated out behind her, swaying in time with the music.

"I have a better idea," Gabby said. "Let's leave it with the presents. Julia will never know who made it!"

From across the room, a man called Daniel's name.

"That's my dad. I've got to go," Daniel said reluctantly.

"Daniel!" his father called again. "Come on!" He held up the dragonfly kite.

"We're going to fly my kite," Daniel told Gabby.

Gabby looked at Mia. "Can I go?" she asked.

"Sure, if Mami says it's okay."

Gabby hesitated. She wanted to go fly the kite. But she didn't want to leave her fairy friends. "Will I see you again soon?" she asked them.

"Very soon," Prilla promised.

"Until next time," Bess said, smiling.

Gabby grinned back. "Until next time," she said. Then she added in a whisper, "In Never Land."

As she set the frog back in the water, Lainey had the feeling she was being watched.

The Never Girls

the woods beyond

Written by

Kiki Thorpe

Illustrated by

Jana Christy

A STEPPING STONE BOOK™

RANDOM HOUSE 🏠 NEW YORK

Chapter 1

Ever since four friends—Lainey Winters, Kate McCrady, Mia Vasquez, and Mia's little sister, Gabby—discovered a secret passage to Never Land, each day held the possibility of a new adventure. Mornings, they woke up feeling like the luckiest girls in the world. Most mornings, that is.

"Lainey!"

Lainey Winters opened her eyes. Her mother was calling her. She reached out, feeling around for her glasses. Her hand touched the wooden nightstand where she always left them.

But her glasses weren't there.

"Lainey!" her mother yelled again. "Come down here!"

Lainey got out of bed. Without her glasses, everything looked blurry. Where could she have left them?

As she fumbled across the room, she stubbed her toe, hard. "Ow!" Lainey cried. Blinking back tears, she hopped on one foot to her dresser and felt around on top. Her glasses weren't there, either.

The bedroom door opened. "Didn't you hear me?" her mother asked. "I've been calling you for the last five minutes." She frowned. "Where are your glasses?"

"I don't know." Lainey looked around helplessly. "Somewhere . . ."

"Not another lost pair," her mother said with a sigh. "You'll have to wear the spare ones."

It was Lainey's turn to frown. She *hated* her spare glasses. Her regular big, square glasses were bad enough. But the spare ones were broken and had been fixed with tape. In Lainey's opinion, they just looked *dumb.*

"When you're ready, come downstairs. There's something I want you to see." Her mother left.

Lainey found the old glasses in her desk drawer. *Why couldn't* these *be lost?* she wondered. Then she got dressed and went downstairs. Her mother was standing in the kitchen with her arms folded across her chest.

"Look outside," she said to Lainey.

Lainey looked out the window. "Oh no!" she exclaimed.

In front of their house, the garbage and recycling cans lay on their sides. The trash bags inside had been ripped open, and garbage was scattered around their yard. More trash was strewn along the sidewalk. "What happened?" Lainey asked.

"Some animals must have gotten into

the trash," her mother replied. "Raccoons, probably. Did you leave those dishes out last night, Lainey?"

She was talking about Lainey's dog bowls. Every morning in the summertime, Lainey filled two big bowls with dog food and water and left them on the sidewalk in front of their house for any hungry or thirsty dogs that passed. Lainey didn't have a dog, but she tried to get to know all the pets in her neighborhood. She liked to help out her furry friends whenever she could.

Lainey's parents didn't share her love of animals. Because they didn't want a pet of their own, they didn't mind the bowls. But the rule was that she had to bring them in at night.

And she *had* brought them in, hadn't she?

Lainey leaned closer to the window. By standing on her tiptoes, she could see down the front stoop. Two metal bowls were sitting by the bottom step—right where she'd left them.

"I'm sorry, Mom," Lainey said. "I guess I forgot."

Her mother sighed. "Sweetie, I think it's wonderful that you want to help the neighborhood dogs. But I told you that dog food could attract other animals, ones we *don't* want around. And now we have a problem. We can't just leave all that trash out there."

"I'll pick it up," Lainey said. "It's my fault. Just please let me keep the bowls."

Her mother considered this, then

nodded. "All right. But you'll need to clean up right after breakfast. You have swimming lessons this morning."

"Swim lessons!" Lainey groaned. That was even worse than having to pick up the trash. Every summer, her mother signed her up for swim classes at the community pool, even though Lainey begged her not to. "But I'm supposed to go over to Mia's this morning," she said.

"You can go to Mia's in the afternoon," said her mom. "You're there all the time as it is. What do you girls do all day? You always come back with leaves in your hair and sand in your shoes, as if you've been trekking to Timbuktu."

Not Timbuktu. Never Land, thought Lainey. But she shrugged and said, "We're just . . . you know, playing."

Her mother smiled and ruffled Lainey's hair. "All right. Hurry and eat breakfast. We have to leave for the pool by nine."

After breakfast, Lainey went outside armed with two big garbage bags and a pair of rubber dishwashing gloves. She looked around at the mess.

Lainey's front lawn wasn't large—just a gated courtyard in front of her row house. But the area was covered with coffee grounds, potato peels, plastic wrap, eggshells, crumpled paper towels, used tissues, and moldy leftovers. More trash was scattered all the way down the sidewalk.

Lainey wrinkled her nose. She wished she could find the animals that did this. She'd give them a good talking-to!

With a sigh, Lainey snapped open a garbage bag and got to work. A slimy head of lettuce brushed against her arm. A milk carton dribbled sour milk onto her jeans.

"Yuck! Double yuck!" Lainey held her breath and kept going. As she worked, she imagined she was already in Pixie Hollow. How much better things were there! She could go for a ride on the back of a deer. Or she could help the herding-talent fairies round up the butterflies. Or watch her animal-talent friend Fawn tend to a newborn fox.

Lainey dragged the full bags back to the trash cans just as her mom came out of the house. "Time to go!" she told Lainey.

A horrible hour of swimming followed. As usual, the pool was too crowded and the water was too cold. The instructor kept telling Lainey to put her face in the water. Lainey was an excellent dog paddler. But every time she dunked her head, she got scared and stopped swimming. It didn't help that all the other kids in the class slipped underwater as easily as fishes. By the time class was over, Lainey was embarrassed, shivering, and miserable.

It was almost eleven o'clock when she got home. Although Mia and Gabby's house was only at the end of the block, Lainey didn't want to lose a second. She ran full-speed and arrived out of breath.

The other girls were in the living room. Pillows were spread out on the floor, and they each stood on one. Lainey saw that they were playing Snapping Turtles, a game Gabby had made up. The object was to jump from one pillow to another to avoid the snapping turtles in the "water"—the floor. Gabby loved the game, but the older girls played only when they were desperately bored.

"Finally!" Kate exclaimed when she saw Lainey.

"We've been waiting for *ages!*" Mia added.

"Mia! You stepped off your pillow!" Gabby cried. "The snapping turtles got you!"

"Who cares?" Mia said, giving her pillow a little kick. "The game is over." She put her hands on her hips. "Where have you been?" she asked Lainey.

"I . . . well, I . . . ," Lainey stammered.

"Why is your hair wet?" asked Gabby.

"Did you just get out of the shower or something?" asked Kate.

"Don't tell me you slept in!" Mia exclaimed.

Lainey's heart sank. Even her best friends were annoyed with her. "I didn't sleep in!" she wailed. "I had swimming lessons. And before that I had to pick up all the garbage—"

"Never mind," said Kate impatiently. "At least you're here now. We can go to *Never Land*." She said the last two words in a whisper.

"Come on," said Gabby. "Let's hurry!"

Lainey's mood lifted as they raced up the stairs to Gabby's room, where the magical passage lay behind a closet door. Visiting Never Land was like opening a present. There was always an adventure waiting. The surprise was finding out what it would be.

It will all be okay now, Lainey told herself as she stepped into the closet. *Everything will be better once we get to Pixie Hollow.*

Chapter 2

That morning in Pixie Hollow, on a high branch of the Home Tree, the fairy Prilla awoke with a start. She looked around her room.

Something had woken her. What could it have been?

Then she heard it. *Crunch. Crunch. Crunch.* The sound seemed to be coming from inside her closet.

Prilla got out of bed and tiptoed across the room. Her closet was a little nook in the wall covered by a maple leaf. She stopped in front of it and listened.

No doubt about it. There was something inside. Taking a deep breath, she pulled back the leaf.

"Ahh!" she screamed. A fat green caterpillar sat in the middle of the closet, chomping on her favorite rose-petal dress.

"Shoo!" Prilla yelled. "Scram!" The caterpillar didn't budge. She threw a slipper at it. The caterpillar ignored her. It finished nibbling a hole through her dress, then started on a tulip skirt.

"Stop, you!" Prilla screamed, throwing the other slipper.

"Prilla? Are you all right?" Beck called through her front door.

Prilla ran to let her in. Beck was an animal-talent fairy. Maybe she could help.

"Hullo!" Beck said when she saw the caterpillar. "How did he get in here?"

"I must have left the window open—Hey, stop that!" Prilla yelled at the caterpillar, who was now nibbling a daisy sundress.

"Shh! Not so loud," said Beck. "Caterpillars don't like loud noise."

"But he's eating my clothes!"

"Well, he's hungry," Beck said. "Can't you see he's about to make a cocoon? That's why he's so fat. He needs a lot of food right now. Don't you, big fella?" She scratched the caterpillar on the back.

Prilla frowned. She'd thought Beck might be a *bit* more helpful. "I'll have to ask the sewing fairies to remake everything," she said.

"They won't be able to make anything

today," Beck replied. "It's Great Games Day."

"Oh no!" cried Prilla. How could she have forgotten? Great Games Day was a rare and exciting event. Fairies of every talent competed to show off their skills. There was a leapfrog race for the animal-talent fairies and an obstacle course for the fast fliers. On the rapids of Havendish Stream, the water fairies held a leaf-boat rodeo. Sewing fairies made fanciful hats, and baking fairies whipped up elaborate cakes. There were poppy seeds to snack on and sunberry punch to drink, and a huge roasted sweet potato for everyone to share. All the fairies dressed up in their best leaf or flower.

And now Prilla's favorite clothes had caterpillar holes in them!

Once Beck had coaxed the tubby bug out the door, Prilla turned back to her closet. The caterpillar had nibbled everything except for one wilted poppy dress in the back.

Prilla had never liked the poppy dress. The sleeves were too tight and the petals drooped. But it would have to do.

It was late by the time Prilla made it to the tearoom for breakfast. Her favorite honey buns were gone, and so was almost everything else. Normally, the baking fairies would have made more. But Prilla knew they were hard at work on their Games Day cakes.

Just as she reached for the last scone, a hand shot out and grabbed it. Prilla turned and saw the fast-flying fairy Vidia.

"Vidia!" Prilla said. "I was about to take that!"

"A bit slow, though, weren't you?" said Vidia. "The quickest hawk gets the mouse, as the saying goes."

"But you have plenty to eat." Prilla pointed to Vidia's plate, which was piled high with breakfast treats.

"Yes, but I need a big breakfast," Vidia replied. "*I'm* competing today. I don't think you can say the same."

Prilla felt her face turn red. Vidia was right. She wasn't part of Great Games Day. Fairies of the same talent always competed against each other, but there were no other fairies with a talent like Prilla's.

Prilla could travel to the mainland— the world of humans—in the blink of an eye and visit children everywhere. She was proud of her talent, for it kept children's belief in fairies alive—and that kept the fairies' magic alive. But sometimes, on days like today, Prilla wished her talent weren't so unusual.

"Well, I'm off to win a race," said Vidia. "Have fun watching." With a swish of her pointed wings, she flew away.

Smarting from Vidia's remark, Prilla sat down at the table. There was hot tea, at least, thank goodness. She poured herself a cup and sighed. *What an awful morning. But I guess that means the day can only get better,* she told herself, taking a sip.

"Ow!" Prilla winced. She'd burned her tongue.

*

After her tea, Prilla flew down to Havendish Stream. All along the banks, fairies were getting ready for the games. The animal-talent fairies were saddling up their frogs. Downstream, water fairies were hoisting their leaf-sails. On the far bank, garden fairies were warming up for the carrot toss.

Watching the excitement only made Prilla feel more left out.

I'll go on a blink, she decided. When she was feeling down, nothing lifted her spirits like visiting children.

Prilla found a quiet spot in the crook between two tree roots, not far from the frogs. She sat down, settling her wilted poppy dress around her. Then she blinked.

In an instant, Pixie Hollow was gone. Prilla was hovering outside a large, white house. Four children in swimsuits were running around in the grass, squirting each other with a garden hose.

Prilla flew over to them. "Clap if you believe in fairies!" she cried.

But the kids didn't clap. They didn't even notice her. They were too busy laughing and running. A girl grabbed the hose and turned it on her friends. They screamed as water rained down on them.

Prilla tried again. She circled above them, saying, "Clap if you be—"

Before she could finish, a blast of water knocked her out of the air.

With a gasp, Prilla was back in Pixie Hollow. By some miracle, her wings were still dry. Otherwise, she was soaked from head to toe, and shivering. But it wasn't from the cold—it was from embarrassment. Those kids hadn't even looked at her!

It was just bad luck, she thought. *The next blink will be better.*

Prilla dried herself off on a dandelion. Then she blinked again. This time she found herself in a wide green field of grass. A group of kids was running toward her.

Prilla smiled and started to greet them. But they ran by without so much as a glance. Then she heard a *thump.* A soccer ball was sailing through the air. It was headed right for her!

In a blink, Prilla was back at the tree root. Her heart was racing. She was furious with herself. Twice she'd blinked—and twice she'd failed.

I should give up, she thought. But that only made her feel worse. Her talent was visiting children—and that was what she was going to do!

Prilla didn't always have control over who she visited on a blink. Usually, that was how she liked it—she met so many more children that way. But now she tried to focus. "Let it be just one kid this time," she said. "Just one boy or girl."

Prilla blinked. She was in a brown room. It had brown curtains, brown carpet, and a brown couch. A young boy lay on the floor with his chin in his hands. He was watching TV.

Prilla flew over to him. "Clap if you believe in fairies!" she exclaimed.

Lost in his show, the boy didn't look up.

Prilla darted in front of his nose. The boy waved a hand, as if swatting a bug. His eyes never moved from the screen.

Tears of anger and frustration sprang to Prilla's eyes. She began to fly circles in front of the boy. "Hey!" she shouted. "Hey! Do you see me?" Prilla waved her hands. She blew a raspberry. She turned a cartwheel in the air.

Finally, she caught the boy's attention. His eyes widened and his mouth formed an O.

Prilla grinned. *At last!* "Clap if you believe—"

"Watch out!" a voice screamed.

Prilla jerked back in surprise. But it wasn't the boy who had cried out. The call had come from far away, in Never Land. Something was wrong.

Prilla snapped back to Pixie Hollow. The scene before her was chaos.

A giant was blundering along the bank of Havendish Stream. Prilla's mind was still on her blink, so it took her a moment to recognize Lainey. The frogs were in a frenzy, hopping up and down the banks as their fairy riders chased after them. Lainey was trying to catch the frogs, too. But she only seemed to be making things worse.

"Don't worry, I've got him!" Lainey yelled as she closed in on a frightened frog.

"Lainey, no!" a fairy cried. But Lainey was trying so hard to catch the frog, she didn't seem to hear.

When Prilla was coming out of a blink, she always felt a bit fuzzy, and she was slow to react. It wasn't until Lainey was almost on top of her that Prilla realized she was about to get stepped on!

"Stop, Lainey! STOP! *STOP!*" Prilla screamed.

Lainey drew up short. Her foot hovered just inches above Prilla.

A look of horror crossed Lainey's face. "Oh my gosh!" she said. "I didn't see you. I'm sorry, Prilla! I'm so sorry!"

Almost getting squished was the last straw. Prilla's bad mood suddenly bubbled over, and she burst out, "Lainey, you must be the *clumsiest* Clumsy who ever lived!"

Lainey looked stunned. She turned and stumbled away.

Prilla regretted her words at once. "Lainey—" she called after her.

But it was too late. Lainey was gone.

Chapter 3

Lainey sat alone beneath the branches of the weeping willow. She hadn't cried once that whole terrible morning. But now the tears flowed down her cheeks.

Everything was wrong. Lainey's bad day hadn't gotten better in Never Land. It had gotten worse—much, *much* worse. To think she'd almost stepped on Prilla . . .

Lainey squeezed her eyes shut. Try as she might, she couldn't erase Prilla's words: "You must be the *clumsiest* Clumsy who ever lived!"

Outside the willow, she heard fairy laughter. Normally, Lainey loved the bell-like sound, but today it made her cringe. Were they laughing at her? By now everyone in Pixie Hollow would have heard what happened. *They're probably all talking about what a big, dumb Clumsy I am,* Lainey thought.

Lainey got to her feet. She couldn't stay here. She wasn't sure she'd ever be able to face her fairy friends again. But where could she go?

The willow room was where the girls had slept their first night in Pixie Hollow. Now they mainly used it as a place to keep things. There were daisy chains Mia had made with the weaving-talent fairies and seashells Gabby had collected on the shores of Never Land.

Lainey spotted her deer harness hanging from a peg on the tree's trunk. The animal-talent fairy Fawn had given Lainey the harness after a particularly rough deer ride.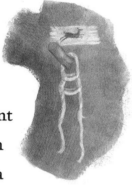

I'll find a deer, Lainey decided. *I'll ride and ride till I'm as far away as I can get.* Just the thought made her feel a little better.

Lainey had never been deer riding without Fawn. In fact, she'd never been in the forest on her own. But that didn't stop her. Grabbing the harness, she ducked outside and looked around.

Just beyond the willow was a deer trail that led into the woods. Lainey followed it. The trail was no more than a matted-down path through the forest undergrowth. It disappeared in some places, only to pick up again in another spot. Sometimes Lainey wasn't sure she was following the same trail, or even following a trail at all. But the woods were quiet and peaceful, and it felt good to walk.

A bird whistled, and Lainey whistled back. She crossed a little stream, where silvery fish flashed in the shallows. Lainey stuck her hand into the cool water and watched them scatter. A tiny frog, no bigger than a walnut, hopped along the bank. Lainey picked it up and cupped it in her hands, feeling its little heart beating.

As she set the frog back in the water,

Lainey had the feeling she was being watched. Slowly, she lifted her head. A black-eyed doe was staring at her from behind the trees.

Her deer! Lainey jumped to her feet. The movement startled the deer and it darted away.

"Wait! Please wait!" Lainey cried, chasing after it.

The doe bounded down a slope. Lainey followed. But she lost her footing on the steep hill. The harness fell from her hand. She tumbled the rest of the way down and landed in a pricker bush.

"Oww!" Lainey tried to get up. Each little movement only made the thorns dig in more. She was stuck!

As she wondered what to do, she heard a voice say, "You're a pudding head!"

Lainey looked around, startled. Through the leaves of the bramble she spied two red, pointed ears. They looked like the ears of a fox.

"If a bear and a lion got in a fight, the lion would definitely win," the voice went on.

"No way!" said a second voice. "I'm telling you, the *bear* would win."

Lainey shifted and caught a glimpse of a rabbit's fluffy white tail.

"Would not!"

"Would so!"

"Would not!"

An electric thrill went through her. All her life Lainey had wanted to talk with animals. She longed to know their feelings and thoughts. And here at last were two she could understand perfectly!

But she was still stuck. Frantically, she tried to get out of the pricker bush. The thorns scratched her skin and tore at her clothes. She could hear the rabbit and fox moving away, still arguing.

Gritting her teeth, Lainey tore herself free. But by the time she reached the place where the animals had been, they were gone.

Lainey stomped her foot in frustration. Where could they have gone so quickly? She began to scour the area for a hole or a burrow, any place an animal might hide.

Not far away was a holly tree studded with bright red berries. There was a hollow in its trunk. *Just the sort of cozy home an animal might like,* Lainey thought.

She went over to the tree and peered inside. The hollow was bigger than she expected. She couldn't see the bottom.

"Hello?" Lainey called. "Anyone there?"

Were her eyes playing tricks on her? Or did she see a faint light somewhere deep down? With her hands stretched out in front of her, Lainey leaned in farther. . . .

She slid down through the tree!

"Oof!" she grunted as she tumbled into a dim chamber.

When her eyes adjusted, she saw that she was in a little room. The ceiling was a network of tree roots. Some of the roots had grown into the room and had been cleverly crafted into furniture. The four posts of the wide bed were made from roots as thick around as Lainey's leg. A washbasin made from a giant tortoise shell was wedged between two roots. Fresh springwater trickled into it from a hole.

A hearth had been dug from the dirt wall. A few coals still glowed inside it—this must have been the light Lainey had seen. In the center of the room was a table made from an old stump. Mushrooms big

enough to sit on surrounded it. Lainey tried a mushroom stool and found it quite comfortable. Bowls made from gourds sat on the table. Lainey peeked into one, but it held only water.

Everything was made for someone just about Lainey's size. It was a wonderfully cozy home, though it didn't seem like the house of a fox or a rabbit. She wondered whose it was.

A terrible thought struck her. What if the house belonged to a troll or some other wicked creature?

She heard voices overhead. They seemed to be just outside the entrance.

Lainey didn't want to be caught standing there. She looked for an escape, but the hollow was the only exit. Beneath the bed, there was a narrow gap between the mattress and the floor. Getting down on her belly, Lainey squeezed into it.

And not a moment too soon. A second later, a furry creature rolled into the room.

It got to its feet and stood with its back to Lainey. Was it a troll? Lainey couldn't be sure. It had fur like a bear. But it stood upright.

Lainey heard a scuffling noise as several more creatures came tumbling down through the tree. As one stood, she caught a glimpse of its face.

Lainey gasped. It wasn't a fox or a bear or a troll. It was a boy!

Chapter 4

There were six boys altogether, dressed in animal skins. Some of them carried clubs or swords. Others carried bows and arrows—not toys, but real wooden arrows with sharp flint arrowheads, the kind Lainey had only ever seen in books.

A boy with green eyes went to the table. "Who's been touching my mug?" he exclaimed, pointing to a gourd.

"Not me," said a boy who was dressed as

a raccoon. He turned to a curly-haired boy in bearskins. "Was it you?"

"Not me," said the curly-haired boy. He questioned a boy wearing rabbit ears in place of a hat. "Was it you?" And on they went, until each of the boys had denied touching the mug.

"Well, *somebody* moved it," said the green-eyed boy.

Beneath the bed, Lainey watched them in astonishment. All along, Lainey had thought that she and her friends were the only children on Never Land. And now to find out there was a whole pack of boys—the strangest boys she'd ever seen!

Just wait till Mia and Kate and Gabby hear about this! she thought.

"Maybe a rat moved it," suggested the curly-haired boy in bearskins.

"I'll get that rat!" said the green-eyed boy.

Lainey inched backward, trying to make herself as small as possible. It turned out to be a mistake. The movement caught the boys' attention.

They drew their weapons. "Come out, rat!" one of them shouted.

Lainey squeezed her eyes shut. She was done for! "I wish I'd never left Pixie Hollow!" she blurted out.

"That doesn't sound like a rat," one boy remarked, lowering his club.

"It doesn't look like a rat, either," said another, peeking under the bed.

The boys bent their heads together to discuss the situation.

"It said it came from Pixie Hollow!"

"It's awfully big for a fairy."

"It's not as pretty as a fairy, either."

"I can hear you, you know," Lainey said.

There was a moment of surprised silence. Then the boys continued their conversation.

"Do you think it might be a pirate?"

"Too small for a pirate."

"It's not as ugly as a pirate, either."

Lainey was getting tired of being talked about as if she weren't there. "I'm not a pirate," she called out. "I'm just a girl."

"What sort of girl?" one of the boys asked. "Mermaid or fairy?"

"Just a regular girl," said Lainey. She crawled out from beneath the bed.

The boys could not have looked more shocked if a talking turnip had popped up from the dirt floor. Their eyes grew round as nickels. Lainey noticed that most weren't much older than she was, and some looked younger. Suddenly, she felt much less frightened.

"My name is Lainey," she said. When

they didn't reply, she prompted, "What are your names?"

The boy wearing rabbit ears stepped forward. "I'm Nibs." He pointed to the tall, green-eyed boy in fox skins. "That's Slightly. The curly-haired one is Cubby. And these two you can't tell apart are the Twins."

A small boy wearing a skunk tail tugged Nibs's sleeve, then pointed to himself.

"Oh, yeah," said Nibs. "And this is Tootles. He doesn't talk."

Lainey laughed at the funny names. "What are your real names?" she asked.

Nibs lifted his chin. "My name's as real as my nose," he replied.

"Sure," Lainey said quickly, not wanting to hurt anyone's feelings. "I just meant, I've never heard names like those before."

"Peter gave them to us," Cubby said.

"Who's Peter?" asked Lainey.

The boys looked shocked. "Peter Pan, of course!" exclaimed one of the Twins. "He's—"

"Our captain!" the other Twin finished.

From the boys' proud faces, Lainey could tell they thought very highly of this Peter. She wondered what sort of captain he was—and what he would think of a girl showing up in his hideout.

As if he'd read her mind, Nibs said, "He's away now. But he'll be back in time for lunch. In fact, we were just on our way to get the rhinoceros."

Lainey raised her eyebrows. "You're having rhinoceros for lunch?"

"Of course not!" Cubby said with a snort. "You can't eat rhinoceroses. They taste awful!"

"We're having coconuts for lunch," Nibs said.

"We need the rhinoceros to ram the tree and knock the coconuts down. *Obviously*," Slightly explained.

"A *real* rhinoceros?" Lainey had never seen a rhinoceros before. Suddenly, she wanted to see this one more than anything. But what if the boys wouldn't let her go with them?

"I can speak Rhinoceros, you know," she said quickly.

That wasn't strictly true, but it wasn't a total lie. Fawn was teaching her to speak (or rather, squeak) Mouse. And while not all animals spoke Mouse, of course,

Lainey had discovered that it was possible to squeak to a bear and make herself understood. She had never met a rhinoceros before. For all she knew, they spoke Mouse fluently.

Nibs looked impressed. "Well then," he said. "You had better come along."

Chapter 5

Prilla stood on a mossy bank above Havendish Stream. Down below, on the mudflats, the leapfrog race was in full hop. Animal fairies seated on frogs jumped over one another. Mud flew as they chased each other toward the finish line.

Fairies on the banks cheered for their friends. But Prilla was only half paying attention. Every so often, she fluttered up above the crowd to look for Lainey. She had been sure Lainey would show up to see her animal-talent friends race. But there was no sign of the girl.

With a last gigantic leap, one of the frogs sailed across the finish line. The rider was so covered in mud, at first no one could tell who it was.

"And the winner is . . . Fawn!" declared the referee.

As Fawn stepped forward to claim her prize, Prilla rose into the air. She would look for Lainey somewhere else.

As she flew, Prilla spotted Kate and Mia crouched beside the stream where the water ran fast. They were watching the leaf-boats dart over the rapids.

"Who's winning?" she asked, flying up to them.

"Rani was in the lead," Mia said. "But her leaf got stuck in a whirlpool. Now it's a tie between Silvermist and Marina."

"Go, Silvermist! Go, Marina!" Kate cried as the fairies flashed by in their maple-leaf canoes.

"I was wondering if you'd seen Lainey," Prilla said.

Before Kate or Mia could answer, Gabby ran up. "I won a prize!" she exclaimed.

"A prize for what?" Mia asked, surprised.

"Pea-shooting," Gabby said. "The garden fairies let me try."

"I thought the games were only for fairies," Kate said.

"They said I was an honorary fairy. I won third place!" Gabby held up a tiny ribbon no bigger than a daisy petal.

Mia and Kate laughed. "Gabby, you're ten times the size of a fairy," Kate said. "You only won third place?"

"I know I'm big," Gabby said. "But *they* have magic." Smiling proudly, she pinned the ribbon to her collar.

"Was Lainey at the pea-shooting contest?" Prilla asked.

Gabby shook her head. "Uh-uh."

"I thought she was at the leapfrog races," Mia said.

"I just came from there. I didn't see her," Prilla replied.

"Come to think of it, I haven't seen Lainey all day," Kate said. "She wasn't at lunch, either."

Prilla wrung her hands. "I'm afraid I might have something to do with that."

She explained what had happened earlier that day. "I didn't mean to hurt her feelings," she told the girls. "I was just scared and upset. I know it wasn't her fault. She didn't see me sitting there."

"I'm sure she'll understand if you tell her you're sorry," Mia said.

"That's what I want to do," Prilla replied. "But I can't find her."

"We'll help you," Kate said. "She must be somewhere around here."

The girls and Prilla looked for Lainey in all her usual spots. They checked the barn where Lainey liked to chat with the mice. They checked the tree where she picked her favorite pink-gold peaches and the mossy rock where she liked to lie on her back and watch flamingos fly past. But there was no sign of her.

As they were passing the willow tree, Mia suddenly had a hunch. She darted inside. The others followed.

"She's not here, either," Mia said as they came in.

"Do you think she went home?" Gabby asked.

Kate shook her head. "I can't believe she would leave without telling us."

"Well, she's not in Pixie Hollow," Mia said. "Where else could she be?"

"Look!" Gabby said suddenly, pointing to the trunk of the willow.

The others looked. "I don't see anything," said Kate.

"That's where her rope thingy usually

is," Gabby explained. "And it's not there now."

"The harness. You're right!" Mia said. "She must be out deer riding."

"By herself?" said Kate. "She never goes without Fawn."

The girls and Prilla looked at each other.

"Something is wrong," Mia said. "Lainey wasn't really acting like herself today."

"I noticed that, too," Kate said. "I wish now I'd asked her why."

"You don't think she's run away, do you?" Prilla asked.

"No," said Kate. "That's not like Lainey."

"She's not that reckless," Mia added, but she sounded uncertain.

"I'm sure she'll be right back," said Kate. "But let's check the forest, just to be sure."

Chapter 6

Lainey and the boys walked along single file. The forest seemed denser here than it had near Pixie Hollow. The air was hotter. The insects buzzed louder. Every now and then, an unseen animal screeched. The sounds made Lainey jump each time.

"How much farther is the rhinoceros?" she asked.

"Just a bit," one of the boys answered.

Lainey swiped a hand across her damp

brow. She was starting to believe that the boys had made the whole thing up and that there was no rhinoceros. Then, suddenly, they came into a clearing—and there he was.

Lainey had seen plenty of pictures of rhinos in books, but none had prepared her for the real thing. He was as big as a bull and looked twice as heavy. His cement-gray skin hung like armor. His tiny eyes sat low on his wrinkled head, which seemed weighed down by its enormous horn.

Lainey thought he was magnificent.

The rhino stood in the middle of a patch of tiny purple flowers. His eyes were half closed. He looked as if he might be dozing. On the other side of the clearing, Lainey spotted a tall coconut palm. Coconuts as big as basketballs hung beneath its leaves.

"What's the plan?" Lainey asked the boys.

From the way they looked at each other, Lainey realized they didn't have one.

"We could dig a hole in the ground and cover it with branches and leaves," Cubby suggested. "When the rhinoceros walks across it, he'll fall in."

"I thought of that," said Slightly.

"But that won't help us get the coconuts," one of the Twins pointed out. "And besides—"

"Wouldn't he notice us digging?" finished the other.

"Exactly my thought," Slightly said, nodding.

"We could light the bushes on fire," one Twin said.

"And drive the rhino toward the tree!" added the other.

"I was just about to say that," said Slightly.

"But we might burn down the whole forest. Including ourselves," Nibs added.

"I knew it wouldn't work," Slightly agreed.

"What if you got the rhino to chase

you?" Lainey suggested. "Then you could lead him toward the tree so he would knock down the coconuts."

The boys thought this was a very clever plan. "Who volunteers?" asked Nibs.

They were all quiet a moment. Then Slightly said, "I volunteer Tootles."

Tootles looked taken aback. He pointed at Cubby.

Then Cubby volunteered Slightly. Slightly volunteered Nibs. And the Twins volunteered each other. Nobody wanted to be the one to rile up the rhino— not even Slightly, who claimed he'd thought of the idea first.

"If Peter were here, he would do it," said one Twin. Everyone agreed it was a shame Peter wasn't there.

Finally, Cubby said, "Why doesn't Lainey do it? After all, she can speak Rhinoceros."

All the boys looked at Lainey. She suddenly regretted her half-truth—which, now that she thought about it, was really more of a lie. But she didn't want her new friends to know she'd fibbed. And she didn't want them to think she was a coward. "Okay," she said. "I'll do it."

The boys all wanted to give her advice on what to say to make the rhino mad enough to chase her, so it was several more minutes before Lainey crept from their hiding spot in the bushes.

She stepped hesitantly into the clearing. The rhino was still sleeping. The only movement was the occasional twitch of his tail.

Maybe I don't need to make him mad, she thought. *Maybe I could just ask him nicely to knock some coconuts down from the tree.*

Lainey inched closer to the rhino. In a voice barely above a whisper, she squeaked in Mouse, "Excuse me."

Quickly, she stepped back, ready to run. But the rhino didn't move.

"Sounds more like a mouse than a rhino," Slightly remarked from the bushes.

"I don't think he heard you," Cubby called to Lainey. "Louder!"

"And maybe less squeaky," Nibs added.

Lainey's palms were sweating. This time, she lowered her voice to a husky squeak. "Hello there!" Her mouth was so dry she had to say it twice.

The rhino snoozed on.

Lainey relaxed. Either the rhino couldn't understand her, or he was sleeping too deeply to care. Showing off a little, she called, "Hey, you with the big beak!" She didn't know how to say "horn" in Mouse.

The rhino didn't even twitch an ear.

Lainey walked back to the boys' hiding spot. "It's no use," she told them. "I think he might be deaf."

The boys didn't reply. They were looking past Lainey with wide eyes. She spun around. The rhinoceros was awake—and he was looking right at her!

For a moment they stared at each other. Lainey took a step backward. The rhino took a step forward.

Lainey bolted—and the rhino charged!
She could hear him thundering after her.
For such a large animal, he was surprisingly fast.

The boys stood by, cheering like kids at a soccer game.

"Thataway, Lainey!"

"Faster, faster!"

"He's right behind you!"

"HELP!" Lainey yelled.

Then something amazing happened. Tootles leaped from his hiding spot. He began to swing his skunk tail and dance around.

The rhino stopped. It turned from Lainey and began to chase Tootles.

"Hey, you, you big lump! Over here!"
This time it was Cubby yelling. The
rhino started to chase him instead. Then
Slightly jumped in to save Cubby. The
Twins jumped in to save Slightly. Nibs
jumped in to save the Twins.

The rhino was getting confused. The
more confused he became, the madder he
seemed to get. Nibs wasn't far from the
coconut tree. But the rhino was quickly
closing the space between them.

"He's not going to make it!" Lainey
cried, covering her eyes.

The sound of the rhino's horn striking
wood rang out across the forest. Lainey
peeped through her fingers. Then she lowered her hands in amazement.

Nibs was sitting high up in the coconut

tree, while the rhino circled below. *How did he get there so fast?* Lainey wondered.

The rhino plowed into the trunk again. The tree swayed. The coconuts trembled. Nibs hung on for dear life.

With a third hit, a single coconut dropped to the ground.

The rhino seemed to feel he'd made his point. He turned and wandered into the forest without a backward glance.

When he was gone, the boys whooped and hollered and slapped each other on the back. Lainey couldn't even smile. It gave her goose bumps to think what a narrow scrape they'd had. She looked at the coconut on the ground. "All that for one lousy coconut?"

"Is that what's bothering you?" Cubby

asked. "Don't worry. Nibs will take care of it."

Sure enough, Nibs was picking coconuts and hurling them to the ground. Then he leaped from the tree. He swooped down as gracefully as a bird and landed next to Lainey.

"You can *fly?*" she asked.

"Oh sure," Nibs replied cheerily. "We all can."

"When we've got fairy dust, that is," Cubby added. "Sometimes it runs out. Then we have to wait for Peter to ask the fairies for more. But he left us with plenty."

Lainey couldn't believe what she was hearing. "Why did we risk our lives with the rhinoceros when any of you could have just flown up and picked the coconuts?"

The boys looked surprised. "What would be the fun in that?" asked Nibs.

Lainey stared at him. Then she started to laugh. "You're crazy," she said.

The boys laughed, too. Then they all sat down for lunch. It turned out to be quite a feast, for there is nothing like being chased by a rhino to work up your appetite. They ate three coconuts apiece.

They sat in the sun, patting their full bellies and talking about who had looked the funniest being chased.

For the first time all day, Lainey felt truly happy.

Chapter 7

"What should we do now?" asked Slightly.

Lainey and the boys were lying in the grass at the base of the coconut tree. They were all feeling sleepy from the sunshine and their big meal.

"How about a swim in the Mermaid Lagoon?" suggested Cubby.

"A swim? Oh no! We can't!" Lainey exclaimed.

"Why not?" asked Nibs.

Lainey thought quickly. "It's just that . . .

you can't swim for an hour after you eat."

Cubby frowned. "Says who?"

"Says my mom," said Lainey. "But every-body knows that. Didn't your mother ever tell you not to go swimming right after lunch?"

"Haven't got a mother," Cubby told her.

"Well, what about your dad?" asked Lainey.

"Haven't got one of those, either," said Slightly. "None of us do."

Lainey propped herself up on her elbows. "Then who looks after you? Your grandparents?"

"We look after each other," Nibs said.

"I don't mean here," Lainey said. "I mean when you go to your real homes."

The boys looked at her blankly. "But this is our home," Nibs said at last.

Suddenly, Lainey understood. The boys didn't travel back and forth through a magical portal. They lived in Never Land all the time.

"So you mean," she said slowly, "that you can do whatever you want? And there are no grown-ups to tell you what to do?"

"That's right," said Nibs. "Whatever we want. Whenever we want."

How wonderful! Lainey thought. No rules or bedtimes. No "dinner before you eat dessert" or "chores before you go out to play." It seemed like the perfect life. How could you ever have a bad day?

"Peter says that grown-ups are like flies on a cake. They just buzz around and spoil the fun," Cubby remarked.

Peter again! Lainey was getting more and more curious about him. "Where is Peter, anyway? Wasn't he supposed to be back in time for lunch?" she asked.

"He did say he'd be back for lunch," Nibs replied. "Though now that I think of it, he didn't say which day."

Even though they'd just eaten, the boys decided to swim anyway. They weren't inclined to listen to the advice of mothers, Lainey's or anyone else's. Lainey felt a knot in her stomach as they walked to the lagoon. She was sure they would laugh her right off the island when they saw what a terrible swimmer she was.

The lagoon was a white sand cove. Big rocks jutted out of the turquoise blue water. Lainey stood on the beach, toeing the sand, as the boys splashed into the waves. She tried to think of some reason why she couldn't go swimming.

I can say my stomach hurts, she thought. *Or my foot has a cramp. Or I'm allergic to water . . .*

Just then, she noticed something. Every boy was dog-paddling. Not one of them had his face in the water.

"What are you waiting for?" Cubby called.

"Come on, Lainey!" Slightly added. "The water's great!"

Lainey kicked off her shoes and waded in up to her ankles. The lagoon was warm as bathwater. With a joyful shout, she splashed in.

They took turns jumping off the rocks and seeing who could make the biggest splash. When they grew tired of that, they

played a long game of keep-away with a sea sponge, tossing it back and forth like a football.

As Lainey dove for a wide throw from Tootles, she suddenly found her head underwater.

She scrambled up to the surface, gasping. Then she paused for a moment, treading water. In the brief seconds she'd been under, she'd caught a glimpse of something amazing.

Did she dare look again?

Screwing up all her courage, Lainey took a big breath and stuck her face into the water. Far out in the lagoon, on the sea floor, was a brilliantly colored coral castle. It had sea-fan curtains and arched doorways. Large fish swam in and out of its open windows.

Lainey was entranced. She lifted her head out of the water, took a breath, then plunged back under to look again.

Nibs paddled over to Lainey to see what she was doing.

"What *is* that down there?" she asked him.

"Oh, you mean the castle? It's where the mermaids live," he replied.

Lainey realized they hadn't seen a single mermaid the whole time they'd been there.

"Where are they all?" she asked Nibs.

"They hide when we come swimming," he replied. "They're snobs that way. Peter's the only one they talk to."

Lainey was disappointed, until she found a starfish on one of the rocks. It was an especially pretty one—purple with green spots. Slightly was sure that a mermaid had worn it in her hair.

"Do you really think so?" Lainey asked, turning it over.

"Sure," said Slightly. "Mermaids always pick the best starfish for their hair. She probably left it behind when she was sunbathing."

Lainey put the starfish back on the rock so the mermaid would find it when she returned. She couldn't help thinking how much Mia would have liked to see the mermaids' castle.

After they'd finished swimming, everyone lay on the sun-warmed rocks to dry off. Nibs went up the beach into the forest and returned with a four-foot stick of sugarcane. He used his sword to cut off pieces, which he handed out.

"Can I see your sword?" Lainey asked as they chewed their sugarcane.

Nibs handed it over. The handle was made of brass and shaped like a dragon. "Where did you get it?" she said.

"From a pirate," Nibs replied.

Lainey raised her eyebrows. "A real pirate?"

"Of course!"

"He gave it to you?"

"Not exactly," said Nibs. "I won it in battle."

"Are there many pirates here?" Lainey asked.

"Sometimes," he replied. "They come and go. Right now they're off the island. Looting ships on the high seas, probably."

A shiver went down Lainey's spine. She wished Kate were there. She knew how much Kate would like seeing a real pirate's sword.

The truth was, Lainey missed her friends. But she was so much better off here. Here she wasn't Lainey-who-always-lost-her-glasses or Lainey-who-made-everyone-wait. And she certainly wasn't the "clumsiest Clumsy who ever lived." She was clever. She was brave. She had faced down a raging rhino and gone swimming in a mermaid lagoon and held a real pirate's sword. She was a girl who could do anything.

"I'm never going back," Lainey said to herself. "Not ever."

Chapter 8

Purple clouds streaked the sky as Prilla, Kate, Mia, and Gabby made their way through the forest outside Pixie Hollow. They had been following the deer trail for some time. But now that the sun had set, the path was harder to spot. No matter how she tried, Prilla couldn't glow much more than a firefly. She wished she'd thought to ask a light-talent fairy to come with them and brighten the way.

To keep their spirits up, Kate began to whistle. Mia joined in. Gabby couldn't whistle, so she sang. Prilla didn't know the girls' songs, so she clapped. Along they went through the darkening forest, walking in single file with Prilla darting among them. Despite the gloom, they made quite a merry little band.

They had just finished "The Hokey Pokey" and were starting on "Jingle Bells" when they heard a low growl.

The girls stopped walking. "What was *that*?" Mia asked.

Kate looked around. "Probably just a dog or something."

"The dogs in *our* neighborhood don't sound like that," said Gabby, huddling close to her sister.

"Prilla, are there dangerous animals on Never Land?" asked Kate.

"There are hawks and snakes, of course. And outside Pixie Hollow the crickets can be real brutes." Prilla shuddered. "No dogs that I know of, though."

"What about anything . . . *bigger*?" asked Kate.

"You mean like bears and wolves and crocodiles?" said Prilla.

"There are crocodiles?" Mia cried, putting an arm around Gabby.

"Just one," said Prilla. "Though he's pretty big."

"I wish we could go back to Pixie Hollow," said Gabby.

"But we can't," Kate replied, saying what they were all thinking. "Not until we find Lainey."

They went on. Kate began to whistle again, but no one joined her this time.

A sudden rustling in the leaves overhead made the girls jump. They stopped and peered up into the trees.

"At least we know that's not the crocodile," Kate said, trying to be cheerful. "*That* wouldn't be in a tree."

"It could be a panther," Prilla said. "I forgot about the panthers."

"Let's keep going," Mia said. "The sooner we find Lainey, the sooner we can get out of here."

They hurried along as quickly as they could, which wasn't very fast at all, since the forest was now quite dark. To lift their mood, Kate said, "Remember Lainey's dog treat stand? It was like a lemonade stand, except she was selling dog biscuits."

"I remember that!" Mia said. "No one in the neighborhood wanted to buy biscuits for their dogs. But Lainey didn't care at all. She just kept giving them away for free."

"She didn't make any money. But she made a lot of doggy friends," Kate said, smiling.

Mia smiled, too. "That's Lainey for you."

"Remember Lainey's first deer ride in Never Land?" Prilla asked.

"I do!" Mia giggled. "She was trying to say 'Giddy-up' in Deer—"

"But she ended up saying 'Fire!'" Kate broke in, laughing. "And the deer just took off! Lainey barely managed to hold on!"

"Remember when she talked to a bear?" Gabby said.

"I heard about that!" Prilla said. "It was the talk of the tearoom for ages. Lainey spoke to the bear in Mouse. What was it she said?"

"She said, 'I'm looking for my brothers and sisters,'" Gabby replied. "And the bear ran away. He thought we were great big mice!"

Everyone laughed.

Suddenly, Kate, who was leading, drew up short. They had come to a thorny thicket. The deer trail was gone. The girls couldn't see any way around or through the snarly plants.

"Now what?" said Mia.

There came a screech from the dark forest. The girls moved closer together. They took each other's hands. Prilla landed on Kate's shoulder.

"I'm sure it's nothing," Kate said uncertainly.

"I wish Lainey were here right now," whispered Gabby.

"So do I," said Mia.

"So do I," said Prilla.

"So do I," said Kate.

Chapter 9

Down beneath the forest floor, a party was taking place in the boys' underground hideout. As a cozy fire crackled in the hearth, Lainey and the boys made shadow puppets on the wall. They held handstand contests and jumped on the bed and tried to scare each other with their best ghost stories.

Lainey was having a great time. But she couldn't stop thinking of Kate, Mia, and Gabby and how they were missing all the fun.

She wondered what her friends were doing. They must have noticed she was gone by now. Were they worried? Had they returned home without her? Lainey was sorry she hadn't thought to leave a note.

Noticing the look on her face, Cubby stopped jumping. "What's the matter?" he asked. "Aren't you having fun?"

"Yes . . . it's just, I miss my friends," Lainey replied.

Hearing this, Slightly and Tootles stopped jumping, too. The Twins and Nibs came out of their handstands. "Were they good friends?" one of the Twins asked.

"Yeah," said Lainey. "And I left without saying good-bye."

"That sounds like a sad story," Cubby said warily.

"Cubby doesn't like sad stories," Slightly told Lainey. "They make him cry."

"Do not!" Cubby shouted, punching him on the arm.

"Do so!" Slightly said, pushing back.

"It's not all sad," Lainey said quickly. "We had lots of fun times, too."

Cubby nodded. "That sounds better."

"What sort of fun times did you have, Lainey?" one of the Twins asked.

They gathered around the hearth to hear the story. Only then did the boys realize that the fire had burned low and they were out of firewood.

They drew sticks to see who would go out to get more. Tootles lost. He gave

Lainey a mournful look, as if to say, "I always lose."

"I won't start the story until you're back," Lainey promised.

Tootles scuttled into the tree, and they heard him slowly climbing up to the forest.

He was gone only a few moments before he scrambled back into the room, gesturing madly.

"Somebody's coming!" Nibs translated. "Pirates, I think. Headed right this way!"

Tootles nodded. The other boys leaped to their feet. "If they've just come back to the island, they'll be looking for a fight," Slightly said.

"A fight with who?" Lainey asked in alarm.

"Whoever they find," Cubby said. "There's nothing like a few weeks at sea to make a pirate mean."

Lainey gulped. It was one thing to hear about a pirate battle. It was quite another to be mixed up in one. "Wouldn't it be better to stay in here, then?" she asked.

"And let them ambush us?" Cubby shook his head. "I say we sneak up on *them* first."

The other boys agreed. They began to gather their clubs and swords.

Lainey was in no hurry to go out into the dangerous night. On the other hand, she didn't want to stay there alone. She watched, uncertain what to do, as one by one the boys headed up to the forest.

Finally, Lainey and Tootles were the only ones left. He looked at her with raised eyebrows as if to say, "Aren't you coming?"

Lainey gazed longingly at the dying fire. How nice it would be to stay in this snug home. But then she thought of how Tootles had rushed out to save her from the rhino. It didn't seem right not to help him—and the other boys —now.

"All right." With a sigh, Lainey followed him, slowly climbing the notches in the hollow trunk that served as a ladder. But by the time she made it up to the forest, the boys, including Tootles, had vanished.

It was a moonless night. The forest was so dark that she couldn't tell where one tree ended and another began. "Tootles?" she whispered. "Nibs?"

Silence.

"Slightly?" she said, inching forward. "Cubby? Twins?"

"Shhhh," said a voice no louder than a mouse's sigh. A hand reached out and pulled her into the bushes.

The boys were crouched together there. They stared into the darkness. Lainey heard a tiny *snap*, like the sound of a twig breaking.

Pirates!

Nibs put a finger to his lips. Then, with a wave of his hand, he motioned the boys and Lainey for-  ward. They began to sneak toward the pirates.

The sound of her own heart pounding filled Lainey's ears, so loud she was afraid the whole forest could hear it. Her eyes had adjusted to the dark now. She could see three figures coming through the trees. They carried a single lantern between them. The lantern flame was so low it cast hardly any light at all.

There's something strange about that lantern, Lainey thought. It didn't swing like a lantern normally would. It moved up and down, this way and that, almost as if it had a mind of its own.

Just then, the light swung up high, and Lainey caught a glimpse of a face. She stood straight up and yelled, "STOP!"

But it was too late. With warlike whoops, the boys leaped out from their hiding place.

The pirates screamed.

The boys screamed, too, and jumped back in surprise. "Girls!" Slightly squealed.

The "pirates"—Kate, Mia, and Gabby— were standing there, clinging to each other in fright. What Lainey had mistaken for a lantern was Prilla, fluttering beside them.

When Kate heard the boys scream, she straightened and peered closer at the furry attackers. "They're not bears," she announced. "They're just boys!"

"I wouldn't say 'just,'" Cubby huffed, drawing himself up with as much dignity as he could.

Kate was about to reply, when she caught sight of Lainey. The girls rushed over to embrace her.

"What are you doing here?" Lainey asked, every bit as surprised as they were.

"Looking for you, of course!" Kate said. "What are *you* doing here?"

"And who are they?" Mia added,

pointing at the boys, who were watching with confused expressions.

Lainey made introductions. The boys were still suspicious. Slightly declared he thought the girls might actually be pirates in disguise. The girls were also wary, since they thought the boys had given them an unfair scare. But when Lainey explained that it had all just been a misunderstanding, everyone warmed up.

Of course, as soon as the girls heard about the hideout, they wanted to see it. The boys, who were proud of their home, were eager to show it off. Kate, Mia, and Gabby tried out all the mushroom stools and looked at the coat hooks and took turns making water run into the washbasin. They praised the boys' cleverness so much that even Nibs turned pink.

As they explored, Lainey told them about her day. Kate was thrilled to hold the pirate sword, just as Lainey knew she would be. Mia was delighted to hear about the mermaid castle. And Gabby liked the story of the rhinoceros so much she made Lainey tell it twice.

In the excitement, Lainey almost forgot about Prilla. When she finally thought to look for her, the fairy was flying out the door.

Chapter 10

Prilla flew into the dark forest. The night air was cool. It felt good after the warmth of the hideout.

She was glad to see the girls reunited, and relieved that everything had worked out. But it had been a long day, and she was eager to return to Pixie Hollow.

Still, she hadn't gotten a chance to apologize to Lainey. The girls and boys had been having such a good time, they hardly seemed to notice her. *Maybe it's better just to leave them to their fun,* she thought.

As Prilla hesitated, she heard footsteps behind her. She turned and saw Lainey. "Where are you going, Prilla?" Lainey asked.

Prilla flew over to her. "Back to Pixie Hollow. But I wanted to tell you that I didn't mean what I said about you being a clumsy Clumsy. I'd fly backward if I could."

"You really didn't mean it?" Lainey asked.

"Of course not!" Prilla exclaimed. "I was just upset. I was having a bad day. The worst day ever, in fact. I'm afraid I took it out on you. Please come back to Pixie Hollow."

"But what about the other fairies?" Lainey said.

"What other fairies?" Prilla asked.

"Everyone," said Lainey. "They must be laughing at me. They think I'm just a big Clumsy."

"No one was laughing at you," Prilla assured her. "I don't think anyone really noticed. They were all focused on the games."

Lainey thought about that. Maybe the fairies she'd heard hadn't been laughing at her after all.

"I'm sorry I almost stepped on you," Lainey said. "You were right to be angry. I should have watched where I was going. I was having a bad day, too. But it's turned into one of the best days ever. Isn't it funny how that works?"

Prilla agreed that it was.

"You know what I think?" Lainey said.

"Maybe bad days are just bad days. It doesn't mean everything is bad."

Prilla smiled. "I think you might be right about that."

Kate, Mia, and Gabby emerged from the hideout, followed by the boys. "Prilla, aren't you staying?" asked Kate.

Prilla shook her head. "It's time for me to go home. It's late, and there's something I still need to do."

"I'm ready to go back, too," Lainey said.

"You're really leaving?" Slightly asked.

"I thought you were going to stay here for good," said Cubby. He looked as if he might cry.

"Thanks, but I miss my home," Lainey told them, realizing it was true.

"But you'll come back for a real pirate battle, won't you?" Nibs asked.

Lainey smiled. "Maybe," she said. "But I might have to miss it. The thing is, I don't speak Pirate."

The boys and girls said good-bye and promised to meet again. Then the girls and Prilla started back toward Pixie Hollow.

"You know," Lainey said as they went along, "there's one thing I'm sorry about."

"What's that?" asked Prilla.

"The boys kept talking about someone named Peter Pan. But I never got to meet him," Lainey said.

"Oh," Prilla replied. "You never know. You still might get the chance. Anything is possible in Never Land."

*

Later that night, Prilla stood on a high branch of the Home Tree. Pixie Hollow was dark and quiet. The games were long since over. The ribbons had all been handed out. The sweet potato had been roasted and eaten. The girls had returned to their homes on the mainland. Now the fairies were tucked in their beds, worn out from the excitement of the day.

Prilla yawned. She was tired, too. But before she went to sleep, she had one thing left to do.

She sat down, settling her dress around her. She focused and took a deep breath. Then she blinked.

She was in the brown living room. The boy was sitting cross-legged on the floor. But this time he wasn't watching TV.

He seemed to be waiting for something.

When he saw Prilla, his face lit up. "I knew it!" he cried. "I knew you were real! I knew it was true!"

Prilla turned a cartwheel in the air, crying, "Clap if you believe in fairies!"

The boy clapped with all his might. Then he held out his hand, palm facing up. Prilla fluttered down and gently landed on it.

The boy brought her closer to his face. She heard him suck in his breath. His brown eyes were wide and full of wonder.

"Fairy," he whispered, "this is the best day ever."

Read this sneak peek of under the lagoon, the newest Never Girls adventure!

Gabby Vasquez soared through the sky over Never Land. The wind blew her hair off her forehead. It whipped the cloth wings on her back, making them flutter like real fairy wings.

Gabby spread her arms wide. She loved flying! Up here she could be anything. She was a giant, with clouds as her ceiling and the forest as her floor. She was the queen of the world! She was—

"Gabby!" Her sister's voice cut through her thoughts.

Gabby looked back. Mia was flying behind her, along with their friends Kate McCrady and Lainey Winters. The fairy Tinker Bell was with them.

"Slow down," Mia called. "You'll miss the turn!"

"No, I won't!" Gabby yelled back. But she slowed down. Together the girls and Tink banked right. As they came up over a crest, a beautiful blue-green lagoon came into view. Looking down, Gabby's heart skipped a beat. They were there!

Mermaids!

They sat together, fanning their tails and combing their beautiful long hair.

Gabby waved to them. The mermaids shaded their eyes and looked up as she passed. But none of them waved back.

The girls and Tink started their descent toward the beach. As Gabby landed, she stumbled in the sand and almost fell. She glanced up quickly to see if the mermaids had noticed. But they were already sliding into the water. Gabby saw the tips of their tails as they slipped beneath the surface.

"They're doing it again!" she cried.

"Who's doing what?" asked Tinker Bell.

"The mermaids! Why do they dive whenever we come? Are they afraid of us?" Gabby asked.

Tink looked at the lagoon. It was empty now. Not so much as a ripple showed that mermaids had ever been there. "No, they're not afraid," Tink said.

"Then why?"

"They're not interested in us," Tink said with a shrug.

"Why not?" asked Gabby. "*I'm* interested in *them.*"

"Trust me, it's better this way," said Tink. "They're not the nicest creatures in Never Land."

Gabby had heard other fairies say this about mermaids, but she never understood why. After all, mermaids were beautiful and magical, like fairies. To Gabby, it made sense that they should all be friends.

"There must be *some* nice mermaids," she said. But Tink had already turned away.

"We're not here to see mermaids, anyway," Mia said. She was helping Lainey pull a deflated raft out of the bushes. "We're here to see *Sunny.*"

Sunny was Lainey's pet goldfish—at least, he *had* been Lainey's pet before she'd accidentally set him free in Never Land and he'd grown—and grown and *grown.* Now her goldfish was as big as a golden retriever! Lainey couldn't keep him anymore, so he lived in the Mermaid Lagoon. The girls visited him when they could, using a raft they'd brought from Mia and Gabby's house.

"First we need to get the raft fixed. There's a hole somewhere," Lainey said, showing the sagging raft to Tinker Bell. Tink was good at fixing things.

Tink flew around the raft, stopping now and then to press one pointed ear against it, until she found the leak. While

Tink patched the hole, Gabby walked around the beach, collecting seashells. There were more—and more interesting—shells here than on any other beach she'd visited. Gabby found several pink scalloped shells, a purple shell shaped like a pincushion, and a long, twisty shell that looked like a unicorn's horn. She put them all in the pocket of her sweatshirt.

A little farther down the beach, she found a bright orange starfish. Turning it over in her hands, Gabby felt a thrill of excitement. She'd seen mermaids wearing starfish in their hair. Maybe this one belonged to a mermaid, too! She imagined the mermaid searching everywhere for her missing hairpiece. How happy she would be if Gabby gave it back! *"It's lucky I found it,"* Gabby imagined herself saying. *"I*

knew you would miss it." And then the mermaid would say—

"Come on, Gabby!"

"What?" Gabby blinked out of her daydream. Mia, Kate, and Lainey were looking at her.

"The raft is fixed. We're ready to go," Mia said.

"I want to stay here," Gabby said. The truth was, she didn't really like visiting Sunny. He'd been cute when he was a little goldfish. But now that he was almost as big as she was, Gabby found him kind of scary.

Mia's brow furrowed. "But we can't leave you alone."

Why did Mia always have to baby her?

Gabby opened her mouth to argue, but Kate spoke up first. "Let her stay. We won't be gone long. She'll be fine on the beach."

"Well, okay," Mia agreed reluctantly. "But don't wander off. And don't go in the water."

"I won't!" Gabby was so happy to be staying that she didn't even mind Mia's bossy tone.

"It's getting late," Tink told the older girls. "I'd go soon if I were you. You shouldn't be in the lagoon after dark."

"Why not?" Gabby asked.

"Full of questions today, aren't you?" Tink said, tugging her bangs the way she did when she was frustrated. "Just be sure to get back soon." With the raft fixed, she said good-bye and started back to Pixie Hollow. Mia, Lainey, and Kate climbed into the raft and paddled out.

Gabby walked along the water's edge,

making footprints in the damp sand. When she got tired of walking, she sat facing the lagoon. She removed her barrettes and tried to put the starfish in her hair, the way the mermaids wore them. But she couldn't get it to stay.

Gabby sighed. She wished she had her bucket and shovel. But she soon noticed that half a coconut shell worked almost as nicely. She scooped up wet sand and piled

it in mounds to make a sand castle.

She'd been working for a while, when a wave suddenly struck her back, soaking her clothes and her wings. Gabby jumped up, startled. She turned to look at the sea. Was the tide coming in? No, if anything the water's edge seemed farther away.

Gabby turned back to her building. She decorated her castle with the shells she'd collected. Suddenly, another wave slapped her, drenching her again. It also swallowed up her barrettes, which had been next to her in the sand.

"Oh no!" Gabby cried. "My barrettes!"

The wave quickly retreated back to the lagoon. Gabby stood with her hands on her hips, glaring at the water. Sunlight sparkled on its calm surface. *Nothing to see here,* it seemed to say.

There was nothing she could do about her barrettes now, so Gabby knelt and began to dig a moat around her castle. But this time she watched the lagoon out of the corner of her eye.

"Aha!" Gabby exclaimed. A finger of water was sneaking up the beach! She jumped back just as it reached her feet. The wave swallowed her sand castle in one gulp.

"Stop that!" she yelled, stomping her foot.

Gabby heard a sound offshore. Or rather, she heard a *not*-sound, like the muffled cough of someone trying not to laugh. Shielding her eyes against the glare, she looked out at the lagoon.

Someone was watching her from between two rocks.